Praise for the Sour Lemon Series

"...a beautiful story with some powerful messages [about] forgiveness and self-discovery."
—Reader's Favorite® 5 Star Review

"...fun and engaging..."
—Victoria Kimble, author of The Choir Girls Series

"Although *Sour Lemon and Sweet Tea* is set in the south, it has universal appeal. It touches on topics such as incomes and outcomes, different definitions of success, sibling rivalry, etc. It's timely, yet timeless. It has sweet ideas peppered with occasional sour grapes, and spicy ideas combined with innocent thoughts. It touches on rich and poor. So pour yourself some lemonade or iced tea and enjoy."
—R. Lynn Barnett, Author of *What Patients Want: Anecdotes and Advice*, and *My Mother Has Alzheimer's* and *My Dog Has Tapeworms: A Caregiver's Tale*

"...engaging and realistic..."-
—KayW., retired school teacher and K-8 school administrator

"My 5th grade daughter and I both read *Sour Lemon and Sweet Tea*. My daughter, who is a 'tween' loved the evolution of the characters in the story. I loved how this book brought me back to how life used to be before technology how children used to grow up playing outside, having chores to do and families coming together at the dinner table for meals. *Sour Lemon and Sweet Tea* makes you really appreciate the simple things in life. I think every ele
would enj
—Good

Sour Lemon Strikes Out

The Sour Lemon Series, Book 2

Julane Fisher

Relax. Read. Repeat.

SOUR LEMON STRIKES OUT
(THE SOUR LEMON SERIES, BOOK 2)
Published by TouchPoint Press
www.touchpointpress.com

ISBN 13: 978-1-946920-61-4
ISBN 10: 1-946920-61-4

Editor: Kimberly Coghlan
Cover Design: Colbie Myles, colbiemyles.net
Cover image: Children sitting in a tree dangling their feet, Brian Jackson, stock.adobe.com

http://www.julanefisher.com/

First Edition

Printed in the United States of America.

For my parents, Gordon and Janet, who taught me the importance of honesty and responsibility.

Chapter 1   Casey

Violet Holt thinks she's the boss of Peachtree Junior High. Considering we've only been in seventh grade for two weeks, I can't, for the life of me, understand why she thinks so highly of herself. She opens her nasty mouth to speak and girls flock to her like ticks to a dog.

"Everyone come over here and get your picture made with me." Violet flips her blond curls over her shoulder and throws her nose toward the sky. "I'll be your next class president."

Della Grayson, Violet's sidekick, is the first to lock arms with her. The rest of the girls squeal and run to her side. Some boy I don't know from the yearbook committee with a camera bigger than his body stands awkwardly in front of Violet.

When I don't move, Violet crinkles her nose like a bloodhound. "Do y'all smell that? That's the smell of a farm girl who bathed in her pigpen all summer."

My face turns as red as a cherry, and my fingers fold into fists. I'm going to punch that smirk right off her face. Before I can step forward, someone grabs me from behind.

"Lillie Mae. Let's walk to class." My twin sister, Ellie, loops her arm through mine and drags me away from Violet before I get in a good left hook.

"But..."

"Let it go, Lil." My brother, Jesse, pulls Ellie and me toward the hallway.

Before we escape the giggling girls, Della spots Jesse. "Hi, Jesse," Della squeals. "Wanna be in our picture?" All the girls cackle.

Jesse groans. "Um, no thanks."

Violet bats her eyelashes at Jesse. "I'm going to be class president. Scrub is taking my picture for the yearbook." She points to the boy behind the camera. He mumbles something, but Violet ignores him.

Jesse smirks. "Don't you think you need to *run* for president before having your picture made?"

Violet giggles. "Of course not. Everyone knows I'll win."

The school bell hasn't even rung, and already, I've had enough of Violet Holt. I let out an exaggerated sigh, turn my back, and walk to class with Ellie.

"Don't walk away from me, farm girl." Violet hates being ignored.

Violet and I have been bitter enemies since she moved to Triple Gap last year. She walked into my sixth grade class like the world should have stopped for her. Della Grayson ate right out of her silver platter. Ellie tried to be nice to Violet though it was no use. Violet hates both of us. The only person in our family she appears to like is Jesse. Then again, all the girls love Jesse.

My brothers, Jesse and Jimmy, are twins in eighth grade. My brother Billy's in fifth grade, and my younger brother and sister, twins George and Grace, are in first grade. Some folks think it's odd to have so many kids, let alone three sets of twins in one family. But I don't know any different, so it doesn't seem bizarre to me.

Before Ellie and I reach the doorway of our math class, my best friend, Mary Olivia Montgomery, yanks me into the room. "Have you seen her yet?"

"Seen who?" I ask.

Mary Olivia throws her hands in the air and lets out a loud puff of air. "The new girl. Casey Culver."

"Nope." I take my seat in the back of the room.

Mary Olivia follows me, beaming like bright lights in a baseball stadium. "She's from Atlanta." She says *Atlanta* like it's a faraway place but it's only forty miles south of Triple Gap. "I think she's a movie star."

I snicker. "Why would she be a movie star?"

"Haven't you heard?" Mary Olivia doesn't wait for me to answer. With stars gleaming in her eyes, she gazes in the distance. "She looks exactly like Daisy Duke."

Daisy Duke is a character from the most popular new TV show of 1979–*The Dukes of Hazzard*. All the girls dream of looking like Daisy with her long, brown curls and tanned legs that go on forever. My brothers drool when she comes on the screen in her short-shorts.

This time, I laugh out loud. Mary Olivia is so dramatic. "I'm sure she's not the *real* Daisy Duke."

Mary Olivia slaps my arm. "Obviously *I* know that. But you should have seen the heads turn when she walked down the hall."

Chuckling, I picture this new girl and Violet together in the same room. "Has Violet met her yet? Sounds like she's gonna have some competition this year."

"I don't know. I can't wait to see what Violet does when she meets her." Mary Olivia throws her head back in laughter, and I join in.

By the time lunch rolls around, all everyone talks about is Casey Culver. "She's so pretty," and "Did you see her hair?" and "She's so tall." All the fuss over one girl has my head spinning. I make my way to the cafeteria as Mary Olivia rushes to my side.

"Come here, Lillie Mae. I want you to meet Casey."

I have no idea how Mary Olivia made instant friends with the new girl in eighth grade. She drags me by the hand to a table buzzing with activity. Standing in the middle of a group of eighth-grade boys is the tallest, most beautiful girl I've ever seen. When she smiles, her blue eyes sparkle. Her perfectly straight, white teeth make me self-conscious of my crooked teeth, and I press my lips together. Mary Olivia was right. She looks like Daisy Duke, minus the short-shorts because everyone knows those aren't allowed in school.

Mary Olivia barges her way to the center of the circle. "This is my best friend, Lillie Mae Liles. Lillie, this is Casey Culver."

When Casey smiles, the light reflects off her white teeth. "Nice to meet you," she says in a high-dollar Southern accent.

Mary Olivia continues to babble. "I invited Casey to come over today. She lives a few houses down from me near the square. You come too, Lillie."

I shrug my shoulders. "I'd rather play baseball. Do you play ball, Casey?"

She shakes her head. "No. I've lived in the city my whole life."

"Have you ever been to an Atlanta Braves game?" I ask.

She shakes her head again. "No."

I stare at her like she's a two-headed calf. *What is wrong with this girl?* "You lived downtown and *never* went to the Braves stadium?"

"No. Guess my family didn't think to take me."

Oh boy. She may be pretty and all, but Casey and I have nothing in common. It won't take her long to figure out she and Mary Olivia are nothing alike either. I'll have my best friend back by the end of the week.

"I gotta get somethin' to eat," I say.

"Okay. You're welcome to sit with us," Casey responds.

"Thanks. Maybe some other time." I spin around on my heels and smack right into Violet. Della trails so closely behind, it's like a train derailing as we pile up on each other.

"Watch where you're going, farm girl." Violet scowls at me and I roll my eyes. Violet spots the circle of babbling boys and heads in their direction until she sees who they're all fussing over. Violet stops dead in her tracks, making Della smash into her again.

Uh oh. Violet's about to throw a hissy fit.

She pushes the boys off to the side and pokes her nosy face into the circle. "Well, I see we have a new girl. I'm Violet Holt."

Casey shows her movie star teeth. "Hi, Violet. I'm Casey Culver. I've heard all about you."

"Of course you have." Violet points her nose toward the ceiling. "I'm going to be your class president."

Casey laughs. "I'm in eighth grade, so I don't think you'll be *my* class president."

Violet looks stunned. "Oh. Well. I meant I plan to run for president. See you around."

I giggle under my breath. No one, and I mean no one, has ever put Violet in her place. Maybe Casey Culver and I have something in common after all.

Chapter 2 Scully

When Violet spots me in the lunch line, she squishes her eyes together and her lips turn downward. After being put in her place by Casey, there is no telling what she'll do. I select a baloney sandwich from the case and step to the cashier.

Violet lets out a loud gasp. "What on Earth do you call that?" She points to the mystery meat in the case. "You'd think with all the farms around here, a girl could get some real meat."

Here comes the hissy fit. While she struts her way through the lunch line, I stand off to one side of the cafeteria by myself, scanning the room for Ellie. I spot her sitting with Mary Olivia's sister, Sarah, and stroll to the table. She and Sarah are laughing.

"What's so funny?" I ask.

"Watching those boys drool over the new girl," Ellie says.

"I think the whole thing is ridiculous." I shake my head and take a bite of my sandwich.

"I've heard she's nice." Sarah drops her head and looks like she's about to cry. "Seems like Freddie thinks so, too. I don't know what to do."

Sarah's had a crush on Freddie Johnson for over a year. Last summer, I tried to explain that Freddie didn't know she existed. Now I feel bad for saying that.

"Boys are so stupid," I say with a mouth full of food. "Not worth having a crush over, that's for sure."

"Stupid, huh?" The loud voice behind me makes me jump out of my seat.

Wyatt Jackson, the boy I've had a crush on since June, stands behind me with his lunch tray. My face heats up, and I worry that red splotches will soon fill my cheeks. Wyatt laughs and drops in the seat next to me. My stomach jiggles. I haven't spent time with Wyatt since that fateful day on my farm last summer when all hope was lost.

A fire destroyed two of our newly built chicken houses. Daddy was bankrupt and thought he'd have to turn over the farm to Duke Holt, until the entire town showed up to help us rebuild.

"I...didn't mean...," I stammer, "that *you're* stupid." My voice cracks. "I was talking about Freddie Johnson."

He gives me a smirk.

Sarah leans in and stares at Wyatt. "How come you're not in the gang of boys over there, drooling over Casey Culver?"

He shrugs. "Not my type." He smiles at me, and I look away, embarrassed. I place my hands on my head and attempt to flatten my brown curls, hoping the humidity outside didn't make them frizz.

Ellie giggles. "Oh, really. So, what is your type?"

I elbow Ellie in the ribs.

Wyatt stares at me. "I don't have a type. I like girls who can speak their mind."

"Lillie Mae definitely speaks her mind," Ellie adds.

This time I punch her, and she shrieks. "Ouch, Lillie." Then she bursts out laughing, and I join in. We both know what's coming next—a twin giggling fit. Once we get the giggles, we can't stop. Right in the middle of the junior high cafeteria, Ellie and I laugh until we're crying.

"If y'all would please stop your giggling fit, I came over to introduce my cousin, Scully Jackson." Wyatt points to a scrawny blond boy that slithered in while I was busy laughing my head off. He has a patch of freckles just below his brown eyes.

"What kind of name is Scully?" I ask, blurting out the first words that pop in my head.

"One my mom thought was cute." He curls his fingers in the air to make quotation marks when he says the word *cute*.

"Geez, Lillie Mae," Wyatt grumbles. "Try being a little nicer. He is my cousin and all."

"It's okay," Scully says. "I get that all the time."

Now I feel bad. "Sorry." I stare at the skinny boy grinning ear to ear. His wavy blond hair curls away from his face. "Wait. You're that photographer from this morning."

"Yep. That's me. Violet called me Scrub. I tried to say my name is Scully, but she didn't hear me."

"She probably ignored you," I snort. "Violet thinks the sun comes up just to hear her crow."

Scully frowns at me. "What does that mean?"

I laugh again. "You're not from around here, are you?"

"Nope."

"It's a sayin' farmers use to describe someone who thinks a bit too highly of himself."

Scully nods. "We have people like that in New York, too."

Ellie's eyes go wide. "New York?"

"Yeah," Scully answers. "I just moved here."

"Did you start school today?" I ask.

"No, I've been here since the start."

I tilt my head to the side. "How come I'm just now meetin' you?" I stuff a bite of sandwich in my mouth.

He shrugs. "Maybe because I'm in eighth grade and we don't have any classes together."

"Why did you move to Triple Gap?" Ellie questions.

Scully points to Wyatt. "Our dads work together."

Wyatt gives a thumbs up. "Yep. My daddy doesn't work for Mr. Holt anymore. He started his own family business with Scully's dad."

"That's probably a good thing," I say, and Ellie gives me a knowing look. "What's New York like?"

Scully takes a bite of his mystery meat. Gagging, he places a napkin over his mouth. "Well, for one thing, we have real meat in our cafeteria. What is this stuff?"

"No idea," I answer, shaking my head.

"It's awful," Scully replies, scooting away his tray. "I lived in upstate New York so it looks kind of like it does here—trees and rolling hills. But New York City is totally different. They have buildings as tall as the sky and people everywhere you look. Cars drive in every lane, honking their horns and shouting out the windows."

Sarah smiles. "I'd like to go there someday."

"You should." Scully smiles. "You'd love it."

"Do you miss it?" Ellie asks.

"Yeah, I do." Scully's smile fades. "But I'm sure I'll like it here, too. What do you guys do for fun?"

"Not much, really," Ellie answers. "Lillie likes to play baseball, but I don't really like it. We work on our farm a lot, and folks go to The Mill every Saturday to swim or fish in the creek." She puts one arm across her chest and rests her chin on her other arm like she's thinking. "That's about it."

"Oh." Scully looks down at his lap.

Before I can ask if he likes to do any of those things, that same big grin makes its way back onto his face. "Well, okay. I guess I'll get used to all that."

He sure doesn't stay upset long. When the bell rings, everyone jumps up to put away their tray.

I wave over my shoulder. "See you around, Scully Scrub."

A smile fills my face.

When I step off the school bus that afternoon, Ellie and I stroll down the long dirt driveway to our house, passing my grandparent's house on the way. Meemaw waves from the front porch, and Pappy looks up from under the hood of his Ford.

"Y'all have a good day at school?" Pappy calls after us.

"Yes, sir," Jesse answers.

"Learn anything?" Pappy asks.

"No, sir." I laugh. I've had this same conversation with Pappy since I started kindergarten.

Pappy chuckles. "Guess y'all should try to learn somethin' tomorrow."

"Good gracious, William," Meemaw complains. "Are ya gonna say that to them every day of their lives?"

"Yep," he answers, winking at me.

"Gonna go play ball now, Pappy," Jimmy shouts, racing ahead.

"Wait for me." I take off, leaving Ellie and Jesse behind.

"See ya," Pappy hollers after us.

I'm out of breath as I plop down on the front porch steps. Jimmy drops his textbooks next to me, grabs his mitt, and races to the pitcher's mound. Jimmy's been our pitcher since I can remember. Daddy taught him to pitch when he was two. He plays on the Triple Gap All-Stars team and will be on the eighth-grade team this spring.

Jesse's our catcher, Billy plays second, and George plays third, leaving me at first base. I march down the first base line as Jimmy pitches a changeup. Grace pops it hard and fast down the middle, taking off like a bolt of lightning. Billy chases the ball, tosses it to me, and I tag Grace.

"Out," Jesse shouts like a true umpire.

"Aw," Grace whines.

"Sorry, Grace." I put my arm around her shoulders.

"It's okay. I should've run faster." Grace has asthma and was so sick last summer, we thought we were gonna lose her.

Mama won't let her play with us much anymore, so I feel bad for tagging her out on the first play.

"Ellie, play for Grace," I shout. "I don't want her to have a coughing fit."

"Coming." Ellie sets her water down and trots to the field. She doesn't like baseball because she'd rather stay clean. But sometimes I con her into playing with me—like I just did. Now, if I can get Casey to play baseball, maybe Mary Olivia would come over here again. That gives me an idea.

"Lillie! The ball," Jimmy hollers. He runs toward me full speed as the ball rolls past my feet. I bend down to pick it up as Jimmy smashes into my back, knocking me face first in the red dirt. Instead of making sure I'm all right, he grabs the ball and tags first base.

"Safe." Jesse waves his hands back and forth, as George glides into first. George jumps up and down, proud of his hit.

Ellie laughs. "You look like a pig in mud."

I stand up and wipe my hands on my white shorts.

"Pay attention," Jimmy growls.

"Geez, Jimmy. You didn't have to knock me over." I wipe my face, but it's no use. I'm filthy and mad.

"Sour Lemon, Sour Lemon," Billy chants from the third base line.

Sour Lemon is the nickname Ellie gave me when we were little because I'm always in trouble. I call her Sweet Tea because there's so much goodness in her. It's one thing for Ellie to say it, but it's a whole other thing when Billy takes to name calling. I try to decide which of my brothers to punch first, and stomp toward third base with my dirty fingers folded into fists. My feet march forward, but Jesse holds my arms.

"Enough, Lil. Get back to first base. Ellie's up to bat." Jesse gives me a shove, then trots off to home plate, squatting down in the dirt.

Grumbling under my breath, I trudge back to first.

"Play ball," Jesse shouts as Jimmy pitches a fastball up the middle. "Strike one."

By the time Ellie strikes out, I'm hot, tired, and grumpy. "I'm taking a break."

"Fine by me," Billy grumbles.

I head to the house to get a glass of sweet tea. As I step into the kitchen, a cool breeze catches the screen door, slamming it shut. "Sorry," I call out to no one in particular. Muffled voices stop me in my tracks.

Last summer, I got myself tangled up like a fishing line in a tree for spying on the grownups. But some habits are hard to break. My mind reels back to all the problems I caused from snooping. And here I am about to do the same dumb thing again.

Placing my back to the wall, I edge closer to the family room and position myself where I can see. I cover my mouth with my hands so my parents can't hear me breathing.

"That's the thing, Tommy Ray." Mama sighs. "Jimmy *is* trying."

"Well, I'm tellin' ya what Coach said. If Jimmy doesn't get his grades up this year and keep them up, he ain't gonna make the eighth-grade team, and he may not make the high school team either."

Uh oh. That doesn't sound good. Jimmy's one of the best ballplayers in the county, but he is *not* good at school. Never has been. The problem is, he's not that smart. I don't say it to be mean—it's simply a well-known fact in my family.

"What if we got him a tutor?" Mama suggests.

"How we gonna afford that, Ruth?" Daddy's voice is edgy. He takes off his ball cap and scratches his head. "We got the farm up and running again, and we don't have money for extras. I'll pull him off the All-Stars team if he can't keep up with school."

Mama is silent so I peek around the corner to see if she's still there. A tear streaks down her cheek. "No, Tommy Ray. We can't take that away from him after the way God provided the money for him to play. I'll ask around. Maybe one of the kids at school can help." Mama puts her hand on Daddy's shoulder and smiles. "He'll be just fine. You'll see."

Chapter 3   Tutor

Today is the fifteenth day in a row Mary Olivia doesn't want to play with me after school. All she talks about is Casey this and Casey that. I'm sick of hearing about that girl.

They've invited me over multiple times to play. But I want my best friend back—without Casey. It's time to have a long talk with Mary Olivia. I dash in the front door and pull the phone receiver off the kitchen wall.

When Mary Olivia answers on the first ring, I blurt out, "Did you think I was Casey calling?"

"Hey, Lillie Mae. No. Casey can't play today."

"Oh?" My lips curve into a sly smile. "Why not?"

"Don't know. She said she was busy and that she'd be home later. She invited me to come over when she gets home."

My heart drops. "Oh."

"Why don't you come too?"

"Because I wasn't invited."

"Yes you are. I invite you to come over every day."

"I know, but I wanna hang out with you. Not Casey *and* you."

"Why don't you like her?" she asks.

I shrug my shoulders even though Mary Olivia can't see me through the phone receiver. "I don't know. She's so...perfect."

Mary Olivia laughs. "Are you jealous?"

"No," I bark. *Uh oh, maybe I am. I'll have to think about that.* "I want my best friend back."

"You're still my best friend. Always will be."

A loud knock at the door startles me. "Hey, I gotta go. Someone's here. I'll call you back later." I hang the receiver back on the wall as Mama opens the front door. Casey Culver stands on my porch with her movie-star smile.

Mama talks a mile a minute, like she doesn't know what to do in the presence of a movie star. "Come on into the kitchen. I thought y'all could work in there."

"That will be fine, Mrs. Liles. Thank you." I try to smooth my frizzy curls. *Too late.*

Casey walks into the kitchen. "Oh hi, Lillie Mae."

"I'm glad to see the two of you have met," Mama says, turning toward me. "Casey's going to tutor Jimmy for a while."

What? Casey is Jimmy's tutor? I nearly fall on the floor. This day just got worse.

When Jimmy struts into the kitchen, he smiles like he got his first tooth. The scent of pine needles makes me gag. Casey covers her nose with her hands.

"Good grief, Jimmy. Did you bathe in Daddy's cologne?" I wave my hands in the air to get the smell out of my nostrils.

Jimmy scowls. "Shut up, Lillie Mae."

Mama interrupts. "Jimmy. I'll let you and Casey get started on reading. Come on, Lillie Mae."

With a smile the size of Texas, Jimmy sits down next to Casey. "Don't mind if I do."

Oh brother. I think I'm going to be sick.

Outside, Ellie sits on the tire swing reading out loud as Grace braids her hair. I fall on the grass next to the giant oak tree and groan. Our cat, Boots, who showed up last summer, rubs against me. We tried to find the owner, but no one claimed her, and she seemed perfectly satisfied staying on our farm. Boots is solid black, except for her four white paws, which Ellie said looked like work boots. The name stuck, and so did the cat. I sit up and scratch her between the ears as she purrs.

Ellie looks up from her book. "Wanna listen?"

"Whatcha reading?" I ask.

"*Little Women.*"

I scrunch up my nose. "That's an old book."

"It's called a classic. Louisa Alcott wrote it in 1868." Ellie gazes toward our house. "It's also one of the few things Mama has left from her mom. She said Grandmother read it to her when she was our age."

Although I'm glad Mama has something special from Grandmother, I sure hope when she passes away she leaves me more than an old book. Ellie picks up her feet, and the swing falls forward.

"Stop," Grace cries, grabbing Ellie by her half-finished braid.

Ellie throws her hand to her hair. "Ouch."

"Stop moving," Grace scolds. Her grownup tone reminds me of Mama.

Ellie stops the swing and points to the cover of the book. "There's something else special about this book, Lillie."

"What?" I stare up at her.

"Y'all have the same middle name. Louisa May and Lillie Mae."

I shrug my shoulders. "So?"

Ellie throws one hand in the air while holding the *classic* with the other. "So, try reading it sometime."

"Reading is boring." I sigh, thinking I have bigger problems to worry about than an old book.

Ellie stares at me like I've lost my mind. "Not if it's the right story. In a book, you get to be anyone you want. You can pick your favorite character and act like that person."

"I'd rather play baseball."

Ellie turns her head toward Grace, and they giggle.

"What's so funny?" I ask.

Grace finishes Ellie's braid and attaches a rubber band to the bottom. "You're like Jo."

"Who's Jo?" I ask.

Grace sighs. "Josephine is the main character in *Little Women*. Ellie, read the pages you read to me." Ellie thumbs through the pages as Grace babbles on about each character in the story. "Ellie's like Meg and Beth combined."

"Sweet Tea?" I interrupt.

"Yeah, sweet and kind, but worried about how she looks." Grace giggles, and I join in. "Amy and Jo bicker all the time."

"They do?" Suddenly, I'm interested.

"Yep." Ellie sits in the grass next to me and reads.

"*Amy teased Jo, and Jo irritated Amy, and semi-occasional explosions occurred—*"

"That sounds about right," I say.

"Wait. I'm not finished yet." Ellie continues to read.

"*Although the oldest, Jo had the least self-control, and had hard times trying to curb the fiery spirit which was continually getting her into trouble; her anger never lasted long, and, having humbly confessed her fault, she sincerely repented, and tried to do better.*"

Ellie sets the book down in the grass and stares at me. "That's you, Lillie Mae."

"No, it's not!" I growl at Ellie.

"Don't worry, Lillie." Grace pats my shoulder. "Ellie says I'm like Amy."

"What's Amy like?" I ask.

"She's a spoiled brat," Ellie offers, throwing her head back in laughter. Grace's jaw drops. "I'm kidding, Grace. You're not spoiled. You're a—"

"Hey," Grace shrieks.

Ellie stands up. "You know I'm teasing you. I'm trying to be like Jo." Ellie pulls Grace into a hug. "Sit down on the swing, and I'll do your braids next." Grace sits, and Ellie combs through her long hair, separating it into two ponytails.

All the screeching makes Boots run behind another tree. I walk to the tree, scoop her up, and nestle her against my chest. "Speaking of brats. Did you see who's inside?"

"Yeah. Casey." Ellie's fingers fiddle with Grace's hair, creating three strands she weaves together.

I let out an exaggerated sigh. "She's Jimmy tutor."

Ellie shrugs. "So?"

"Now I have to see her at school *and* at home. I can't get away from her."

Ellie turns her head to the side. "Why do you want to? She's not a brat. She's nice."

I blow a puff of air. "Nice? She stole my best friend!"

Ellie laughs. "No one stole anyone. You worry too much, Lillie."

"Yeah, Lillie. Worry, worry, worry." Grace giggles.

I reach over and tickle Grace, making her pull away from Ellie.

"Stop," Ellie scolds. "Now I gotta redo her braid."

Setting Boots down, I lie flat on my back as the smell of freshly cut grass fills my lungs. "No one plays baseball anymore. Jimmy's too busy making googly eyes at Casey, and Mary Olivia won't play baseball because Casey doesn't."

Ellie shrugs her shoulders again and ties off one braid. "Play ball with Billy and Jesse. Or invite Betsy over. She's a good friend, and you haven't seen her since our birthday party."

"It's not the same," I complain. "Why do new people have to move to town, anyway?"

Ellie laughs. "Not everyone who's *new* is bad. Like you and Scully. Y'all are friends. Maybe even more than friends." Ellie wiggles her eyebrows up and down, trying to make me laugh. It always works. No matter how hard I try to act mad, giggles escape out of my mouth.

"That skinny scrub? Nah. Just friends."

Ellie's smile turns to a mischievous grin. "I think he likes you."

My eyebrows shoot up. I leap off the ground with a new energy. "Maybe he'll help me."

"Help you with what?" Grace asks.

A smile spreads across my face as I run to the house, a plan formulating in my mind.

Chapter 4   Plan A

"Hey, Scully." I run to his locker where he spins the lock around and around. When it doesn't open, he bangs on the locker, and the metal echoes down the hall. I laugh. "Can't get it open?"

He runs his hands through his blond, wavy hair and scrunches his brow. "No. It gets stuck every time."

I push Scully aside and place my right hand on the dial. "What's your combination?"

"22. 14. 5," he recites.

I spin the dial as he spits out each number. The locker pops open on the first try.

Scully's eyes go wide. "How did you do that?"

I throw up my hands. "Easy."

"Yeah, for you," he grumbles. Scully pulls out his camera, placing a new roll of film inside.

"Can I ask you something?" I swallow hard.

Scully winds the film around a hook and snaps the back of the camera shut. "Shoot." He laughs at his own joke, pointing to his camera.

I try not to roll my eyes. "What would you do if someone stole your best friend?"

He burrows his eyebrows together. "Depends. Does your best friend still want to be friends with you?"

"Yes."

"Then no one has stolen her. She's distracted." I don't say anything. "Is this about you-know-who?" He nods down the hall, and I follow his gaze. A group of giggling girls with a tall brunette in the middle march toward us.

"Yep."

"I wouldn't worry about it if I were you. She'll be gone before you know it."

"What do you mean gone?"

He tilts his head to the side. "No one can be popular forever."

Scully might have given me the perfect plan.

At lunch, I march to Violet's table where her following has dwindled to just one. Nodding to Della, I stare at Violet.

"Well? What do you want, pigpen?" She narrows her eyes.

My face heats up, and I almost change my mind. Instead, I hold my ground. "You and I both know you hate Casey Culver."

Violet glares at me. "So. What's it to you, farm girl?"

Ignoring her insult, I press on. "What if there was a way to make her move back to Atlanta?"

She squints her eyes. "Why do you care?"

"Let's just say, we both would benefit." Violet doesn't answer. "So? Are you in?"

She points her nose to the sky and slings her blond curls over her shoulder. "What do you have in mind?"

My face curves into a slight smile.

"I wanna come over and hang out with you and Casey today," I announce to Mary Olivia as the dismissal bell rings.

Mary Olivia follows me to my locker. "Really? I'm so glad. You're gonna love Casey. You'll see."

Yeah, we'll see all right. "I gotta ask Mama when I get off the bus, but she'll probably say yes. I'll call you." I wave as she skips toward Casey.

Mary Olivia looks back over her shoulder and smiles. "See you soon."

I step off the school bus and drag Ellie down our driveway. "I'm going to Mary Olivia's to hang out with Casey."

Ellie smiles. "What made you change your mind?"

"I'm pretending to be friends with Casey," I whisper.

Ellie stops and glares at me. "Why would you do that?"

"Because I need to convince her to run for school president. The principal told Violet there could be only one president at school. That means even though Violet's in seventh grade, she can win, and everyone knows she's gonna win. Duke will see to that."

"Why would Casey care if Violet wins?"

My hands fly in the air. "No one can be popular forever," I say, quoting Scully.

"What's that supposed to mean?"

"Casey's the most popular girl in school right now. Losing to Violet will be so embarrassing, she'll wanna change schools—or better yet, move back to Atlanta."

Ellie frowns. "That's your plan to get your best friend back? You're sticking your nose in a bee's nest again, and you're gonna get stung even worse this time. Haven't you learned your lesson?"

Maybe Ellie's right. I got stung bad last summer by sticking my nose in others' business. But this time is different. This is a matter of life and best friends.

I don't answer Ellie. Instead, I head inside. "Mama," I say in the sweetest tone I can muster. "May I please go to Mary Olivia's house today?"

"As soon as you complete your chores."

"Yes, ma'am." I drop my backpack in my room as Ellie marches my way.

"I don't like it one bit," Ellie scowls, "and I won't support you. That's mean, and you know it."

Ellie always tries to be good. Sometimes I think she'd have a lot more fun if she were bad once in a while.

"That's why you're not comin' with me," I retort. "I'm gonna get my chores done."

I stomp down the hall, slam the door, and head up the hill to the garden. I scan the soil for ripe vegetables, but don't see any. Running to the chicken houses, I grab a load of fresh straw to put down in C house. Our chicken houses have letter names. A house, B house, all the way to F house. Seven houses in all that I have to help keep clean.

Jesse's already knee deep in straw by the time I reach D house. "Hey, Lil. I got this part done already. You start over there." He points to a brood of hens.

For reasons I can't begin to understand, these horrid hens are fond of pecking at my legs. I hate them. I point my pitchfork at a hen I'm certain is ready to attack. "Any hens wanna come after me today?"

Jesse laughs. "At least you're learning how to fight back instead of running like a scared rabbit."

"Ha, ha." I roll my eyes. Jesse sprinkles new hay behind me. "Can I ask you something?" I don't wait for him to answer. "What would you do if someone stole your best friend?"

Without a single beat of hesitation, Jesse blurts out, "I'd pray about it."

"I should've known," I mutter under my breath.

Jesse pushes his shoulders to his ears. "What? I would. You should too. It's like this, Lil. God answers our prayers when we ask. Sometimes he answers with a loud yes and you get your way. But other times he makes us wait."

"Why?"

Jesse throws his hands to the sky scattering hay across the barn. I sneeze three times. "I think 'cause he wants to teach us a lesson." He stares at me. "Maybe there's something you're supposed to be learnin' in all this."

Chapter 5 Class President

When I arrive at Mary Olivia's house an hour later, she answers the door dressed like she's going to a funeral.

"Good grief, Mary Olivia. Who died?" I bark.

She bursts out laughing and holds the screen door open for me. "Me and Casey are taking pictures. We're gonna tell everyone at school tomorrow someone asked us to be on the set of *The Dukes of Hazzard*. Think they'll believe us?" She laughs again. "Casey is Daisy Duke, and I'm playing the part of a woman trying to lead Bo Duke astray."

"How? By making him wanna go to a funeral too?"

Mary Olivia giggles. "My character recently lost her husband, so I'm in mourning. I'm also filthy rich, so Bo Duke won't be able to resist me."

"Where do you get these ideas?" I ask.

Mary Olivia points to the magazine on the coffee table. "From the *TV Guide* magazine." Right there on the cover, staring back at me are Bo, Luke, and Daisy Duke. Mary Olivia opens the *TV Guide* and reads the episode description. "It says right here, 'a rich widower attempts to lead Bo Duke astray, and Daisy tries to stop him.'"

"Who's dressing up like Bo?" Before she can answer, I peek my head around the corner where Scully Scrub stands in a pair of tight blue jeans with a plaid shirt unbuttoned to his navel. My brown eyes go wide, and my jaw drops to the floor. "What in the world?"

Scully lets out a loud laugh. "Can you believe Mary Olivia talked me into doing this?"

Seeing Scully dressed like that was too much. My entire body fills with giggles, and my laughter hits the others like a tidal wave. We laugh so loud, Mrs. Montgomery runs into the room to make sure we're all right.

Once I'm over the shock of Scully, I glance at Casey and wonder why I hadn't noticed her sooner. Casey has on a pair of blue jean shorts chopped shorter than my brother Billy's buzz cut. My mouth hangs open as she ties her plaid button-down shirt into a knot at the front.

"Who do you wanna dress up like, Lillie?" Mary Olivia interrupts my gaze and sticks her face in front of mine. She grins ear to ear. "Why don't you be Sheriff Roscoe P. Coltrane and pretend to arrest me?"

The thought of dressing up like a ridiculous cop has me wishing I were back home getting pecked by chickens. But since I'm already pretending—pretending I like Casey, pretending I want to be her friend—I stay quiet and play along.

We spend the next hour looking through magazines to be sure our costumes appear *authentic*. Mary Olivia stresses the word *authentic* over and over as if anyone will believe we were on the set of the show. I just want to talk to Casey and go home.

Mrs. Montgomery snaps a bunch of pictures with Scully's camera, then ushers us to the front porch where she places four glasses of sweet iced tea. Casey sits in a rocking chair with her back toward me. After several minutes, I get the courage to talk to her.

"Casey?" She turns to face me, and I use the sweetest voice I can muster, doing my best to sound like Ellie. "I was thinking. Why don't you run for school president? You know, against Violet? It would grate on her nerves to know you're gonna run too."

Casey laughs. "Violet sure doesn't like to share attention, does she?"

"You have no idea." Mary Olivia shakes her head, and her hair flies in her face.

"So, what do you think?" I smile and pretend I'm holding a giant poster. "I can see it now. Casey Culver for President!"

"No thanks." She laughs. "I'm not interested in that kind of thing."

Scully frowns at me. "Why do you want Casey to run for President, anyway?"

Gulp. "Um, I think Casey would make a great president," I lie.

"Me too," Mary Olivia pipes in, smiling. With Mary Olivia on my side, my plan may work.

Casey shakes her head. "No. I don't think so. Thanks for thinking of me."

Ugh. This girl is difficult.

Spending the next few days with Casey gets me nowhere. She won't run for president against Violet no matter what. According to Casey, if Violet wants to be president that bad, she can have it.

On Saturday, as my family piles into the back of our Chevy truck and heads to Sawnee Feed and Seed, I try to focus on how to get my best friend back.

When we pull into the gravel parking lot, my family scatters in all directions. I hop out of the truck and step inside the building to look for Uncle Chicken. Uncle Chicken's the owner of Sawnee Feed and Seed, which everyone refers to as The Mill. He's also the smartest mathematician I know. He can formulate numbers in his head up to the billions and spit out an answer before anyone has time to blink. I make it my business to come up with crazy math problems to see how long it takes him to give me an answer.

"Well, if it ain't the old twin," he hollers, spotting me coming in the door.

"I'm not old yet, Uncle Chicken," I say.

He chuckles his silent laugh. "So, whacha got fur me today?"

I take a deep breath, hoping I can finally stump him. "Ready? What is four thousand, eight hundred and fifty-seven times nine thousand, four hundred sixteen?"

He rubs his hand on his chin like he's thinking hard, then he spits out an answer before I have time to say all done. "Forty-five million, seven hundred thirty-three thousand, five hundred and twelve." He smiles, revealing his toothless gums.

"Dang. How do you do that?" My mouth hangs open wide enough for a bird to fly in and build a nest.

Uncle Chicken nods his head. "School, Lillie Mae. Ya gotta stay in school."

He always says the same thing to me. "I will. I promise," I say, giggling. Tilting my head to the side, I press my lips together. "Uncle Chicken, do you know the Culver family?"

"Can't say I do. They farmers?"

I shake my head making my braids fly in my face. "Nope."

"Well, reckon I only know the farmers in town. Why ya askin'?"

I fiddle with a piece of hay sitting on a nearby crate. "I want to know why they moved here."

His eyes narrow. "Yur not thinkin' of stirrin' up trouble, are ya?"

"Who, me?" I stick the hay between my teeth, turn my head sideways, and bat my eyelashes.

Uncle Chicken doesn't smile. "Now, ya listen here, Lillie Mae. Leave well enough alone."

I drop the hay on the ground. "What does that mean?"

"Means don't go stirrin' up trouble when trouble ain't there." He sets his hand on my shoulder. "Ya hear?" It's not really a question.

"Yes, sir," I say, hanging my head. Then, I look up and grin. "But if you hear anything about them, will you let me know? Please?"

Uncle Chicken takes his hand off my shoulder, turns around, and walks away without a word. Maybe talking to Uncle Chicken wasn't such a good idea after all. As Mama and Daddy select the feed they want, I head down the hill to search for Mary Olivia. Spotting her wading at the edge of the creek, I sneak up behind her.

"Boo."

"Lillie Mae. Why do I let you scare me like that?" She gives me a gentle push.

I shake my head. "I've been asking myself the same thing for years."

"Take your shoes off and come in with me."

"Okay." Pulling one shoe off, I look around. Seems like almost everyone is at The Mill today. Everyone except Casey that is. A grin fills my face.

Billy and George cast a line upstream. Ellie and Sarah stand on the shore near Freddie. Poor love-struck Sarah can't stop smiling at Freddie. Jimmy and Jesse toss a baseball with Tift Johnson and shout at Freddie to hurry.

"Where's Casey?" I ask, slipping off my other shoe.

"Her daddy's not a farmer."

"Yeah, so?"

She shrugs. "She didn't wanna come."

Stepping into the cool stream, I shiver. "Not even to play in the creek?"

"Nope."

I wrap my arms around Mary Olivia's waist. "I get you all to myself for the day."

Mary Olivia smiles. "Come on. Let's go sit in the creek." She runs to a set of nearby rocks where the flowing water makes a peaceful sound. I sit in the water and let the cold liquid pour over my shoulders.

"When are you gonna come over and play ball?"

Mary Olivia looks away. "I don't know."

"How about Sunday, after church?"

"I'm going to Casey's for lunch."

I burrow my eyebrows together. "Monday after school?"

Mary Olivia stares at the water. "Me and Casey are going shopping with her mom."

"Oh." I sink underwater and scream. When I open my eyes, Mary Olivia stares down at me, and I sit up. "You don't wanna hang out with me anymore, do you?"

"Yes, I do. I don't want to play baseball though."

"Why?"

Mary Olivia doesn't look me in the eye. "I don't really like it anymore."

I sigh. "Because Casey doesn't?"

"Yeah. No," she stammers. "I guess I'm growin' up, Lillie. I like girl things now, like shopping and dressing up and fixin' my hair."

My eyes fill with tears. "Like Ellie," I mutter under my breath.

"It doesn't mean we're not friends."

"But it means we're not *best* friends anymore." I run off before she can respond.

Chapter 6 Spying

When we arrive home from The Mill, Daddy drops us off at the barn to unload the straw and feed. I move in slow motion, carrying one bale of straw at a time. The whole way home, I tried to hold back my tears. Now, they race down my cheeks.

Ellie wraps her arm around my shoulder. "What happened?"

I recite my conversation with Mary Olivia, fully expecting Ellie to cry with me. Instead, she laughs. "You're so silly. You're still her best friend. We're best friends, and I don't play baseball."

"That's different. You're my twin, so you have to like me." I put my head down so my brothers won't see my tears.

"I don't *have* to like you. I choose to." She wiggles her eyebrows up and down. "You can be friends with someone even if you're different from them. You don't have to like the same things all the time."

"Mary Olivia says she likes dressing up and putting on makeup because Casey does."

Ellie shrugs. "So? Why don't you try doing the things they like? Then later, invite them over here to do the things you like."

Grumbling under my breath, I pick up a bale of hay. "I'd rather get rid of Casey."

I carry the hay to the back of the barn. Mama and Daddy stand outside talking about Jimmy. The wooden walls have holes the perfect size for spying, so I sneak to a back corner of the barn below the loft and pretend to straighten the bags of feed. Daddy's voice grows louder.

"What do ya mean he got an F on his test? I thought the tutor was helpin'?"

Mama pats Daddy on the arm. "She is, Tommy Ray, and her name is Casey." Mama sighs. "But it's going to take time to see results."

"Jimmy doesn't have time. He's gotta pass now to make the team in the spring. I think all he's doin' is staring at that girl. He's got a crush the size of the Blue Ridge Mountains."

Mama grins and winks at Daddy. "Reminds me of you when you met me."

Daddy laughs. "Can't disagree with you there."

I press my eyes against the wooden slats to get a better look. Mama gives Daddy a kiss on the lips. My eyes go wide as I look away.

"We need a boy tutor so he can concentrate." Daddy rubs his fingers through his hair.

"The only reason he agreed to the tutoring is because of Casey. Take her away, and he'll really fail."

A rustling noise startles me and I whip my head around.

"What do you think you're doin'?" Ellie glares at me.

Gulp. I've been caught spying. "Shh." I put my finger to my lips, and climb out of my hiding spot, crouching down on the barn floor. "Promise me you won't tell. They're talking about Jimmy. He's got a crush on Casey."

Ellie rolls her eyes. "Duh. That's obvious."

I slap her arm. "Hush, so we can hear what else they're sayin'."

"No. I won't eavesdrop, and neither should you." Ellie stands up.

"Fine. I never will again. But for now, could *you* please be quiet so *I* can hear?"

Ellie storms off as I press my eye against the hole in the barn wall.

"How much we payin' that girl, anyway?" Daddy growls. "We can't afford to throw money away."

Mama kisses Daddy on the lips again. "One more month of tutoring, Tommy Ray. Okay? I'll be sure Jimmy pays more attention to the lesson than the tutor."

Daddy mutters something under his breath and steps around the corner. That's my cue to move before I get caught. I dash toward the barn door and smash into Ellie.

"Mama and Daddy kissed on the lips. Twice." I giggle.

Ellie wiggles her eyebrows up and down and smacks her lips together, making kissing sounds in the air. I bust out laughing. It feels good to laugh after being upset about my best friend. By the time Daddy comes inside to see what the ruckus is about, I lie in the hay with tears of laughter streaming down my cheeks, and Ellie is face down in the straw trying to suppress her giggles.

"Back to work, girls. Now," Daddy growls. Ellie and I stand up and walk outside, continuing to giggle. "Since y'all can't get control, you earned yourselves some extra work. Go on out to the garden. Grab a hoe and a shovel."

That stops my giggles right then and there. I open my mouth to complain as Ellie clamps her hand down hard on my lips. "Yes, sir," she replies.

Why do I have to live on a farm?

Chapter 7   Sundays

In my family, rain or shine, snow or hail, Sundays are for church. Last year, Mama decided it was time for Ellie and me to dress up proper, like the other ladies at church. Mama believes a true Southern lady should always wear hosiery with a dress. I hate dressing up. The hosiery is hot and itchy. I tug and pull to get them on, wiggling like an inchworm trapped in dirt.

"Ugh," I screech as I pop a hole with my fingernail. "I did it again." A snag trickles down my leg.

Ellie sighs. "I've shown you how to do it a hundred times. You're too impatient."

I take off the ripped pair and throw them in the corner of the room. "Why can't I wear shorts?"

"A true Southern lady wears hosiery," Ellie says in her best impression of Mama.

"That's correct, Ellie," Mama replies from the doorway. Ellie's face turns as red as a raspberry. "Lillie Mae, hurry up and get dressed so we're not late for church."

"Yes, ma'am."

Grace appears behind Mama. "Need help, Lillie?"

"Yeah. I need a new pair of hose." I point to the wad. "Those are goners."

"Again?" Grace asks.

Ellie laughs. "My thoughts exactly."

I roll my eyes. "Could someone please just get me a new pair so I can get ready?"

Grace goes to my drawer and pulls out a pair of black hose. "Here you go."

"Black? I'm going to Sunday school, not a burial." I stand up, select a white pair, and pull them on the way Ellie showed me.

"Hi, Lillie Mae." Scully waves as I walk down the aisle at church.

"Hey, Scully. You comin' to our Sunday school class today?"

"Yeah. Wyatt's told me all about Miss Marsh." He and Wyatt exchange grins.

I scrunch my eyes together. "You like Miss Marsh too, Wyatt?"

"Nah," Wyatt answers. "Wanted to give Scully somethin' to look forward to."

I laugh. "Better watch out 'cause Jesse's got a crush on her bigger than Sarah's hair." The three of us turn around, and sure enough, Sarah's hair sticks up higher than our barn roof.

Mrs. Buzby pounds on the organ keys signaling everyone to take a seat. She must have forgotten to turn on her hearing aid because the organ is so loud, I have to cover my ears. Pastor Eddie rushes to the organ and turns a knob. Mrs. Buzby stares straight ahead at the sheet music, singing at the top of her lungs. Her singing is enough to make a dog howl.

I sit in our pew next to Ellie. My family has sat in the same pew since the turn of the century. That's how it is at our church. Everyone sits in the same row their whole life, and no one dares venture out. My family is so big, we take up two pews in church. It's totally embarrassing.

When Pastor Eddie dismisses us, I dash to Sunday school. Ellie, Sarah, Mary Olivia, and I always sit together. Even though I'm upset with Mary Olivia, I still want her next to me. When I get to our row, Scully is sitting in *my* seat.

Wyatt comes up behind me. "Mind if we sit with you, Lillie Mae?"

I don't know what to say. I like him and all, but taking my seat in Sunday school is annoying.

"She doesn't mind a bit," Ellie answers. She scoots down to make room for them.

"Sure. I guess," I manage to get out. I'm so embarrassed. *Since when do I care so much about tradition?*

When Miss Marsh steps in front of the class, I glance at Scully. He's grinning ear to ear. Looks like Jesse has competition. "Today, we're talking about friendship. Paul and Barnabas were good friends and worked together. One day, they had a big disagreement that could've ended their friendship. We're going to read about how they handled it."

Miss Marsh seems to be speaking right to me, and I wonder if she knows about my friendship troubles with Mary Olivia.

Jesse raises his hand. "Miss Marsh. This is from the book of Acts, right?"

Miss Marsh smiles. "Yes, Jesse. That's correct."

Jesse puffs up his chest like a peacock. I roll my eyes, and Scully laughs out loud. Then Wyatt snorts. Oh boy, Miss Marsh is losing control of the boys. She continues teaching for twenty minutes, until the snickering gets so loud, she can't get a word in edgewise.

Miss Marsh throws her hands up. "Let's end here. Perhaps we can pick up where we left off next week."

Someone should've prepared poor Miss Marsh for junior high boys.

Mary Olivia grabs my arm before I can stand up. "Lillie. Will you go shopping with me and Casey this week? Please?" she begs. "It'll be fun. You'll see." When I don't respond, she continues babbling. "Okay, listen. If you do this for me, I promise I'll come play baseball with you."

My eyes light up. "Really? Okay, deal."

"Deal it is." Mary Olivia grins.

"What's the deal?" Scully asks.

"Lillie Mae promised to go shopping with me and Casey, and I promised to play baseball with her."

"Sounds fun," Scully responds. "Well, the baseball part I mean."

I smile. "You can come too."

He grins. "Really?"

"Sure." I shrug.

"Okay. When?" Scully asks.

Mary Olivia looks at me. "Next Sunday?"

"Perfect." I smile. Things may be looking up.

Chapter 8 Failing

As the school bus rolls into the parking lot, Ellie turns toward me. "Whatcha smiling about?"

"I'm going shopping today after school with Mary Olivia and Casey," I answer.

Ellie steps off the bus. "That's good. Right?"

I step down, too. "I guess. I'm glad Mary Olivia invited me but..." I pause.

"What?" Ellie asks.

"I wonder why Casey moved here."

She gives me a weird look. "What do you mean?"

Ellie and I walk to our lockers. I open mine and pull out my science book. "I mean, she must not be that smart if Jimmy's still failing. She's been tutoring him for a month. Wonder if she failed out of private school."

Ellie elbows me in the ribs. "Where did you hear that?"

"I didn't hear it anywhere."

"Well, don't go sayin' things like that. That's like spreading rumors."

"I'm not spreading rumors." I curl my fingers to form quotation marks. "I'm *sharing*." That's what the ladies at church call it because gossiping in church is wrong. "Anyway, it seems weird she moved way out here in the country."

Ellie glances toward Scully who shuffles toward us. "People have different reasons for moving. Take Scully, for instance. His daddy moved all the way from New York so he could build houses here. Come to think of it, isn't Casey's dad a builder?"

"Yep. Engineer. He builds bridges."

"Well, there you have it. Triple Gap's got more roads goin' in than any other county north of Atlanta. We won't be a farming town forever."

"I should hope not," Violet interrupts, sticking her nose in the air. "The smell around here is enough to make my hair droop." She glances behind her. "Isn't that right, girls?"

Della stands behind Violet, but there's no one else around. "Don't you mean, girl?" I nod my head toward Della. Ellie snickers. Down the hall, a flock of gaggling girls follows Casey to class.

"Shut up, farm girl." Violet scowls.

Scully appears at his locker, beaming as usual. The camera hanging around his neck fills his entire body. He fiddles with the flash before snapping a picture of Ellie and me.

"Howdy, y'all," he says, in the most atrocious Southern accent.

Ellie and I burst out laughing. "Where did you hear that accent, Scully?"

"TV." He shrugs his shoulders. "Where else?"

"It's horrible," Ellie says.

"Yeah, well. I'm trying to be Southern like y'all." He drags *y'all* into a three-syllable word.

"Why would you want to smell like a pigpen?" Violet sneers.

Heat rises to my cheeks. I've had enough of Violet for one day.

Ellie grabs my arm and tries to drag me down the hall. "We need to get to class. Don't we, Lillie Mae?" It's not up for discussion.

Violet's frown turns to a smirk. "Excuse me, Ellie. I need a word with your twin sister."

Ellie stares at me, and I shrug my shoulders like I have no idea what Violet wants. "Go on, Ellie. I'll catch up." When Ellie is out of earshot, I turn to Violet. "What do you want?"

"What you promised me. You said Casey would run for class president, and when she loses, she'd move away."

"No deal. Casey said if you want it that bad, you can have it."

"That's not good enough. You better come up with another plan. What have you found out about her?"

"Nothing," I bark.

"Nothing?" She scowls.

"Nope. All I know is she's been tutoring Jimmy for a month, and he's still failing. Daddy's gonna fire her if Jimmy's grades don't improve." I look down at the science book I'm holding.

"Interesting," Della remarks, speaking up for the first time.

"Yes. Quite interesting," Violet agrees. "Wasn't she in a private school in Atlanta?"

"Yep," I answer. "One of the finest private schools in the city. Expensive too."

"Maybe she failed out," Della suggests.

I look at her in surprise, wondering if she overheard me say that to Ellie. "Who knows?"

Violet smiles an evil smile and she reminds me of the Grinch when he got the idea to steal Christmas presents from the folks in Whoville. "Yes, perhaps she did."

Suddenly, I get the feeling I said too much. "I gotta get to class."

As I turn around, Violet grabs my arm. "Don't forget, farm girl. We had a deal."

Chills run down my spine.

Chapter 9 Shopping

After school, Mary Olivia and I walk with Casey to her house. Casey opens her front door, and the scent of something sweet drifts toward me. When we reach the kitchen, Mrs. Culver stands next to the stove. She is tall and pretty, with brown hair pulled back in a barrette. Her pantsuit fits her like a glove, and she wears a pearl necklace with bits of diamonds surrounding the white beads. Now I know where Casey gets her looks.

"Mom, this is Lillie Mae."

"Nice to meet you, Lillie Mae. I'm glad you joined us." Mrs. Culver's smile lights up her face.

I'm at a loss for words. "Thank you."

"I baked chocolate chip cookies for a snack," Mrs. Culver says. "Here, Lillie Mae. Have one."

She places the warm cookies on a plate. When I pick one up, the gooey chocolate oozes through my fingers and I lick them clean.

I smile. "Thank you. Chocolate chip is my favorite."

"As soon as you girls finish, we'll go into town to see what we can find." Mrs. Culver wipes the kitchen counter and places the cookie sheet in the sink.

"What are we shoppin' for?" I ask, with a mouth full of cookie.

Casey and Mary Olivia exchange looks, then giggle. "Nothing. We like to look around and try clothes on for fun," Casey explains.

"Oh," I say, feeling stupid. In my family, the only reason we go to a store is if we need something. I'm not allowed to touch anything for fear Mama would have to pay for it.

"Was I supposed to bring money?" My face heats up, and I wonder if I have red splotches on my cheeks.

Mrs. Culver pats my shoulder. "Not at all, Lillie Mae. We want you to have a good time." She smiles, and I relax. Mrs. Culver slings a fancy, designer handbag over her shoulder. "Ready?"

I stuff the rest of my cookie in my mouth and wipe my face with the back of my hand. I wish I could take some with me.

"Yes," Mary Olivia answers, jumping up from the kitchen table. "Come on, Lillie Mae. Let's go."

After locking the front door, we stroll down the street to the square, passing Mary Olivia's farm. As cars bustle past us, I imagine I'm in Atlanta, walking downtown and seeing all the sights.

"I love Sawyer's," Casey says, interrupting my thoughts. "It reminds me of a gift shop in Atlanta, near my old house. Mind if we go there first?"

Sawyer's Gifts and Market is one of the oldest stores on the square. Mr. Rumsfeld, the owner, went to school with my parents, and he inherited the store from his father.

I'm surprised Casey asks me for permission.

"Um, that's fine," I manage to say. *Why would she even ask?*

When I step inside Sawyer's, I head to the jewelry counter and stare into the case. Spotting a ruby necklace, I grin. It reminds me of the necklace Ellie got for her birthday.

"You like the jewelry?" Casey stands next to me, peering down into the glass case.

"Yeah. I always wonder what it would look like on my Mama."

"Really? That's sweet." I frown, wondering if Casey is making fun of me. "I mean most girls would want it for themselves. You think about others a lot, don't you?"

Suddenly, I feel awful for wanting to get rid of her. "Not really. Ellie is the sweet one between us. You'd probably like her a lot better than me. She calls me Sour Lemon."

Casey laughs. "I don't think you're sour. I like both of you. You're both nice."

I swallow. "Thanks. I guess."

"Lillie! Casey! Come here," Mary Olivia beams with excitement. She points to a shirt filled with sparkle and strokes the fabric. "Isn't it beautiful?"

Mama's voice rings inside my head. *Don't touch a thing.* The voice is so strong, it forces me to keep my hands down at my sides. *Ellie would be proud of me for following the rules.*

"Try it on in the dressing room," Casey tells Mary Olivia. "Then come out and show us."

For the next fifteen minutes, Mary Olivia and Casey try on hats and scarves, and place handbags on their shoulders. Finally, Mrs. Culver pushes us out the door.

"Where should we go next, Lillie Mae?" Casey asks.

I don't want to tell her I've never shopped anywhere else on the square. The only reason I'm allowed in Sawyer's is because Mr. Rumsfeld buys vegetables from my Mama.

"You decide," I reply, breathing a sigh of relief.

"Okay. Lennard's it is," Casey replies. *Oh, no.* Lennard's is high-end fashion. I can't even afford a hanger in that store. "It reminds me of the Rich's department store downtown. Have y'all ever been there?"

Mary Olivia answers, and I'm grateful. "No. The only other person in Triple Gap who shops there is Violet."

"Oh. In that case, let's not talk about Rich's anymore." Casey smiles.

I'm beginning to like this girl. Grinning to myself, I walk inside Lennard's and stare at the golden chandelier hanging at the entrance. Its crystals catch the light, casting stars on the wall. The color-coordinated clothing hangs on white silky hangers.

"Good afternoon, Margaret." The sales lady smiles. Seeing how she knows Mrs. Culver by name, I suspect this is not Casey's first trip to Lennard's. Suddenly aware that my mouth hangs open, I press my lips together.

"Good afternoon. I brought the girls to browse."

"Wonderful," she replies. "Please let me know if I can help."

I look down at my outfit. I'm so embarrassed I want to run away. My shirt and matching plaid shorts are from a yard sale. I don't remember the last time I had a new outfit. The only new things I have on are my Nike sneakers I got for my birthday last July.

Mary Olivia slips her arm through mine. "It's my first time in here too," she whispers, smiling.

A sigh of relief escapes my lips and I feel better already. "Should we try something on?"

"Yeah. If our Mamas were here right now, there's no way we'd be allowed to touch, let alone try on. Let's pretend for one day we have all the money in the world."

I beam. "That sounds fun."

Mary Olivia and I select the most expensive outfit we can find. I pick white bell-bottom pants with a gold belt, and a shiny gold top. I rush to the dressing room. When I step out, Casey gasps.

"Lillie. You look—"

"Like you could be in the movies," Mary Olivia finishes, and Casey nods in agreement.

I look ridiculous. "Don't you two get any ideas of me dressin' up to be on a fake movie set again," I tease, giggling like a schoolgirl. Here I am, trying on expensive clothes and acting like I'm a rich kid from Atlanta.

"All right, girls. It's time to go," Mrs. Culver calls into the dressing room.

When we enter the bright sunlight, I smile at Casey. "I had so much fun. Can I come with y'all again sometime?"

"Of course." Casey smiles her million-dollar smile.

Mary Olivia puts her arm around my shoulder. "See. I told you we're still best friends."

I'm as happy as a dog chewing a bone. When Mrs. Culver stops to talk to a lady I recognize from church, I walk backwards and bump into someone. As I turn around to apologize for my clumsiness, I come face to face with Violet.

"Well, well. Look who we have here," Violet sneers.

"What do you want, Violet," I bark.

She whispers in my ear. "Hey giggly farm girl. Friends with the private school dropout?"

"Shut up, Violet," I shriek, pushing her away. I want to smack that smirk right off her face.

"What did she say, Lillie?" Mary Olivia asks.

"Nothing," I shout. "Let's go."

But Violet stands in our path, with her Grinchy evil grin. "It's good to see all the girls in Triple Gap having such a good time together. Oh, how fun."

Mary Olivia rolls her eyes and lets out an exaggerated sigh. "Bye, Violet."

When we walk away, my smile fades. Casey pokes me. "Hey, Sour Lemon. Why the frown?"

Mary Olivia bursts out laughing. "How did you know her nickname?"

Casey smiles and points to me. "She told me."

Grinning, I laugh too. At least for now.

Chapter 10 Baseball

As much fun as I had shopping with the girls earlier this week, I'm glad to be back where I feel the most comfortable—on my baseball diamond. After church, I change out of my Sunday clothes faster than a cat chasing a mouse. I grab a ball and glove and race for the field. The hot sun feels like heaven on my back as I toss the ball with Jesse.

"So, you like her now?" Jesse asks, referring to Casey.

"Yeah. She's nice."

"We've been tryin' to tell you that."

I grin. "Sometimes I can be a little stubborn."

"Sometimes? A little?"

"Hey." I throw the ball hard, hitting him on the arm.

"Ouch."

"Oops. Sorry, Jesse." I didn't mean to hit him.

He moans and rubs his arm. "What position should everyone play?"

I shrug. "I don't know. You decide."

Jimmy races to join us, scoops the ball, and tosses it over his shoulder. "Who's comin' today?"

Before I can answer, Mary Olivia's truck rolls down the driveway, slinging chunks of red clay. When the door opens and Casey steps out, Jimmy's eyeballs fall out of their sockets. Casey wears a pair of cut-off jean shorts and a T-shirt with her hair pulled back in a Braves baseball cap.

"Good grief, Jimmy. Put your eyes back in your head," I bark.

Ignoring me, Jimmy saunters to greet Casey. "Hey. Comin' to play ball with us?"

"No, Jimmy. She's dressed like that to go to church," I holler.

Jimmy scowls at me before turning his attention back to Casey. "What position do you wanna play, Casey?"

She shakes her head. "I don't know. I've never played before."

Jimmy grins ear to ear. "In that case, I'll teach you."

I think I'm going to throw up.

Stepping onto first base, I punch my fist into my glove. Jimmy winds up and throws a curve ball.

"Strike one," Jesse bellows from behind home plate.

Scully's up to bat, and Tift offers tips on how to swing. Before I know what's coming, Scully hits a hard ground ball my way. I reach down to scoop it up and trip Scully. He falls facedown into the dirt.

I panic. "You all right?"

Brushing dirt off his pants, he stands up. "Is this how you greet all your visitors?"

"I'm sorry, Scully." I blush. "It was an accident."

His smile returns. "I know. I was messing with you."

I push him sideways with the ball still in my glove.

"Out," Jesse shouts.

Tift tosses his hands in the air. "What? How's that fair? She knocked him down."

"Yeah, then she tagged him out," Jesse answers. He's always looking out for me.

"Oh, come on," Tift yells.

By the time Casey's up to bat, Jimmy throws the ball underhand.

"What's that, Jimmy?" Freddie mocks from the dugout. "Goin' soft on a girl?"

Jimmy grins real big. "Ready, Casey? Now, hold it the way I showed you."

Ellie giggles and I join in. Ellie and I are about to have a giggling fit right in the middle of our baseball game. I'm so busy cackling, I don't see Casey whack the ball, sending it flying to the outfield. My jaw hangs open as Casey flies past me toward second base. Billy, who's waiting on second, stares as Casey runs to third. Now it's up to George to stop her. He catches the ball and tags her.

"Safe!" Jesse flails his hands back and forth, crisscrossing them along the third base line. Everyone cheers.

Jimmy throws his cap on the ground and scratches his head. "I thought you said you've never played before?"

Casey grins. "Well, that may have been a *bit* of an exaggeration."

I laugh so hard, my belly aches. We all laugh. Who would've thought a girl like Casey Culver, the movie star from Atlanta, would be a natural at baseball?

I think I made another best friend.

Chapter 11 Boots

Jimmy and I bolt for the door at the same time. "Hi, Casey," I grin, reaching the doorknob first. Jimmy scowls at me behind the door. I step aside to let her in. "Jimmy's right here waitin' on you."

"No I'm not," Jimmy barks.

Casey peers behind the door, smiling her movie-star smile. "You're not standing there or you're not waiting on me?"

Jimmy stammers. "I'm...never mind." He stomps toward the kitchen leaving Casey and me giggling.

It's kind of funny I don't mind having Casey here anymore. In fact, I'm excited about it. As we step into the kitchen, Jimmy sits at the table pouting. He doesn't even smile at Casey. Maybe I just crumbled his crush.

"If you have time after you're done tutoring Jimmy, I'll show you around the farm. I mean, if you want to." My words get jumbled in my mouth.

"I'd like that." She gets a funny look on her face.

"What?" I ask, cocking my head to the side.

"It's just that, well, I've never actually seen a real chicken before."

Jimmy and I exchange startled looks. "Never?" Jimmy raises one eyebrow.

Casey shakes her head. "No."

I smile. "You'll see so many here, you probably won't care if you ever see another one as long as you live."

She laughs. "Okay. See you in a few."

I stroll outside, stopping at the tire swing where Ellie and Grace wait.

"Well? What did she say?" Ellie gives me a sideways glance.

"She wants to stay and look around. Can you believe she's never seen a live chicken?"

"I can believe it. She's from the city," Ellie says.

Grace shakes her head. "That's sad."

Ellie tilts her head sideways. "Bet Scully's never seen one either."

Frowning, I squish my lips together. "You're probably right."

"I'll invite him over later so you can give him a tour." Ellie bobs her eyebrows up and down.

"Stop, Ellie. I told you we're just friends."

"Uh, huh."

"Lillie and Scully sittin' in a tree. K-i-s-s-i-n-g," Grace chants.

"All right. That's it. You're in for it now, Grace Ann." She squeals as I chase her off the tire swing, around the huge oak tree, and pull her into a hug. I tickle her until she can't breathe. "Say it, Grace. Say you're sorry."

"No," she squeals and darts toward the house. I pretend I'm mad at her as we run in the yard, playing chase. Eventually, she gets tired and trots off to practice cartwheels.

When Casey and Jimmy come outside thirty minutes later, Ellie and I follow them up the hill to the hen houses.

"We have seven houses," I explain, pointing to the low-lying buildings. "My grandfather, Pappy, gave them each a letter—A through F. Kind of dumb names if you ask me."

"See those two?" Ellie gestures to the wooden buildings furthest away from us. "Those are E and F house. A bad storm last summer destroyed them."

Casey glances at Ellie. "Is that when the families in town came to help you rebuild?"

"Yeah. Did Lillie Mae tell you about that?" Ellie asks.

"No. Mary Olivia did. People around here sure are nice. Help each other and stuff. That didn't happen much where I lived." She gazes in the distance, and her smile fades. Before I get the chance to ask her about it, she perks back up. "So, this is A house?"

"Yep. This is it." Jimmy swings the door open, and the smell fills my nostrils. Casey's hands fly to her face, and she gags.

Ellie rests her elbow on Casey's shoulder. "We forgot to warn you about the smell."

"I'd say so," Casey answers, through clasped hands.

Jimmy shrugs his shoulders. "You get used to it."

I shake my head. "No, you don't."

As the horrid hens rush toward me, Casey shrieks and jumps backward. "I hate when they charge at me like that." Pointing to my legs, I scowl. "I've been pecked more times than I can count."

"All right. Enough of that. You've seen one chicken, you've seen them all." Jimmy slams the door. "See you around. I gotta get to work." He shoves the sleeves of his shirt up and tightens his muscles.

Once he's out of earshot range, I fire away. Using my best boy voice, I grunt, "I gotta get to work. See my muscles?"

Casey bursts out laughing. "That's a pretty good impression."

"I've had a few years to work on it. Boys are so stupid." I laugh. "Hey, Ellie. I'm gonna take Casey to our swing. Wanna come?"

"Nah. I'm gonna see if Mama is back from the Johnson's farm yet. I'll catch up with you later."

"Okay." I wave. "Come on, Casey."

We head back down the hill to the oak tree nestled next to my house. Casey climbs up the tree after me to my favorite branch where we dangle our legs above ground.

"I can finally breathe," she says, taking three deep breaths of clean farm air.

"You think that's bad? You should smell the farms where they keep the chickens in cages. Now that's bad." I scrunch my nose together and wave my hand back and forth in front my face.

Casey pinches her nose. "I never want to raise chickens."

I laugh at her joke, then scrunch my eyebrows together. "I've been wondering. Why did you move to Triple Gap?"

"My dad was hired to build the interstate bridge over the lake, so we moved here."

"Oh." I pause, not sure how to ask her about something she said earlier. "So, how come folks didn't help where you used to live?"

Casey stares in the distance. That's the second time today she's had that expression. "I didn't want to be different, but some kids thought I was a freak because—"

"Lillie Mae!" Grace charges toward us. A fearful expression fills her face. She bends over out of breath and places her hands on her knees. "It's Boots," she says between breaths. "Something's wrong."

I hop out of the tree and charge to the red barn. Grace kneels on the barn floor and points to Boots underneath the loft. "She won't come out." Her voice crackles.

"So?" I shrug.

"She's panting like she can't breathe," Ellie answers. "I think something's wrong with her."

Boots is curled into a ball, and when I stick my hand in, she swats at me. "Looks like she wants to be left alone." I glance at Casey. "She showed up last summer during that storm, and when no one claimed her, we kept her."

"Why did you name her, Boots?" Casey asks.

"Because of her four white paws." I point to Boots who stands up as if she knows we're talking about her. She walks in circles like she's chasing her tail. "See, she feels better already."

Ellie shakes her head. "I don't think so. I think she's sick or something."

Grace looks up, tears in her eyes. "She's been in here all day. She keeps doing that circle thing and makes weird noises."

"Maybe you should go get your mom." Casey's face matches Boots' paws.

"Good idea." Ellie scurries off with Grace following close behind.

Casey sits down on the barn floor and peers in. "Hi, Boots," she says in a high-pitched baby voice. "I sure hope you're not sick. Even if you are, I'll help you get better." She reaches in, and Boots rubs her head against Casey's hand.

I stare, dumbfounded. "She likes you."

"I know what's it's like to be sick." Casey looks away, her expression hard to read. For once, I don't pry. When she turns back around, tears spill onto her cheeks.

"Are you all right?" I ask.

She wipes her cheeks with the back of her hand. "I have leukemia, Lillie Mae."

"Leu what?"

A slight grin fills her face. "Leukemia. It means cancer."

I feel horrible for asking. "Oh. I'm sorry."

"It's okay. I'm doing good now." Casey pauses, taking a deep breath. "I was in and out of the hospital so much the past two years, I got behind in school. When my hair fell out, kids were really mean. Made fun of me and stuff. So, I never went back."

"You never went back to school?" I ask in surprise.

Casey shakes her head. "Not to my private school. I enrolled in classes to catch up. Just because my hair fell out doesn't mean my brains did." She glances my way and smiles. "My mom thought it would be good to move here so

I could get a fresh start with kids who treat me the same as everyone else."

I thought about all the times I harbored hate toward her and wanted her to move back to Atlanta. I feel horrible for having those nasty thoughts. "I'm sorry," I say again.

She shrugs. "It's different than living in the city, but I like it here. Everyone's nice."

Not everyone, I think to myself, hoping she never finds out about my plan to get rid of her. I need to tell Violet I don't want to partner with her anymore.

"Please don't tell the other girls yet. I'm not ready for everyone to know."

I nod my head. "Okay," I say, wondering why she told me instead of Mary Olivia.

Ellie and Grace march into the barn, holding Mama's hands. Casey and I move backward to give Mama space. She squats down and peers in the corner, as Boots paces back and forth, panting like she's out of air. "Well, I'll be."

"What, Mama?" Grace frets. "What's wrong with her?"

Mama smiles, and her eyes light up. "Boots is going to be a mama."

We all stare at her. Grace speaks first. "Huh?"

"Boots is having kittens," Mama exclaims.

"Kittens?" I squeal.

Ellie's jaw drops. "*That's* what's wrong with her?"

Mama laughs. "Grace, go get a blanket out of the closet, and Ellie, grab some towels."

"When will they be born?" Casey asks.

"Depends. Within the next few hours, though, for sure." Mama whispers to Boots the way she does when Grace is having an asthma attack. "It's all right, girl. Won't be much longer now."

"What can I do?" I ask.

"Go get her some fresh water to drink," Mama replies.

I dart out of the barn, Casey on my heels. Grabbing Boots' bowl, I turn on the water spigot attached to the side of the barn.

"Can I stay and watch?" Casey asks.

"If it's okay with your mama." I shrug.

"Can I use your phone?"

"Sure. Ellie will show you where it is." Casey skips down the hill to my house.

A few minutes later, Ellie, Grace, and Casey return with towels and blankets and drop them next to Mama. Everyone crouches down near Boots.

"Are they here yet?" Grace paces back and forth.

Mama laughs. "No, silly. It doesn't happen that fast."

"My mom said I have to go home." Casey's face droops. "I wish I could stay."

My face fills with a smile. "Come back tomorrow."

"Really?" she asks, surprised.

"Yeah. You and Mary Olivia rush over here after school. Mama, will the kittens be born by then?"

"Yes, definitely." Mama fluffs the blanket one last time. "There. She'll be comfortable now. Let's give her some space. We can check on her later."

We send well wishes to Boots, and head toward the house as Mrs. Culver pulls in our driveway.

"See you tomorrow," Casey shouts over her shoulder, running to her mom's car.

I can't believe I ever hated that girl.

Chapter 12 Kittens

Before bed, Ellie and I head to the barn with Mama one last time. A loud howling makes me stop in my tracks. "Boots?" Bolting up the hill, I fly into the barn. Boots licks herself, cries, then licks herself again.

"What's wrong with her?" Ellie's eyes fill with tears.

"Nothing's wrong," Mama says, rounding the corner. "She's trying to have her babies."

"Why is she howling?" I frown.

"It's all perfectly normal, Lillie Mae."

"So, she's not in pain?" Ellie whispers.

Mama hesitates before answering. "I think she's just fine. Aren't you, sweet girl?" Mama slides the water bowl toward Boots.

"Does she need more food?"

"Not right now, Lillie Mae. She's not hungry. Once the kittens are born, though, she'll be starving." Mama turns around to face us. "Girls, you need to get some sleep."

"I can't possibly sleep." Ellie opens her eyes wide. "What if she needs us?"

"I'll check in on her later tonight." Mama stands up and smiles ear to ear. "Don't worry, Ellie. This is exciting!"

"Yeah, Ellie. Don't *you* worry. That's my job." I giggle.

Ellie laughs. "Isn't that the truth!"

My eyes fling open the next morning, and I climb down the ladder. I open my dresser drawer and grab a shirt and a

pair of shorts, not caring whether they match. I have no idea
what time it is.

"Ellie. Wake up," I whisper.

Ellie moans as Grace rolls over in her bed. "It's dark
outside."

"I wanna see if the kittens were born. You comin' or not?"

"Yeah." She rubs her eyes and slides the dresser drawer
open, careful not to wake up Grace.

When we reach the kitchen, Mama sits at the table, a
cup of steaming hot coffee between her hands. Spotting us,
she smiles. "You're up early."

Ellie yawns. "What time is it?"

"Five forty-five," Mama replies.

"Were they born?" I ask, excited.

Mama yawns next. "Yes. Go see. Don't touch them
though."

I march toward the door, then stop and turn around.
"Were you there when they came?"

Mama takes a sip of hot coffee and nods her head. "Yes.
She did great."

"Were you were up all night?" Ellie asks, holding the door
open for me.

"Not all night. Only until I was sure she was going to be fine."

My face fills with happiness. "Let's go."

When Ellie and I step into the barn, the first thing I hear is
squealing. Resting on the blanket, curled into a pile are four tiny
kittens, all different colors. Not able to contain her excitement,
Ellie jumps up and down, pulling me with her.

Grace sneaks up next to us. "Ellie! There's four kittens!"

"I see them." Ellie turns toward Grace and frowns. "Wait. What are you doin' up?"

"Y'all are loud enough to wake the neighbors. How am I supposed to sleep with all that racket?"

Ellie laughs and grabs Grace's hands, jumping up and down with her. "Isn't this exciting?"

Grace squeals like a kitten, and I smile. I haven't been this happy in a long time.

When I step off the school bus the next day, I head straight home to do my chores. I stir the litter in the hen houses without complaining and check on the garden. Seeing only a few pieces of ripe corn, I throw them in a bucket and head back down the hill.

Within minutes, Mrs. Montgomery drops off Mary Olivia, Sarah, and Casey. As we head up the hill to the barn, I spot Freddie, Tift, Short Stop, and my brothers following us. They're probably more interested in Casey than the kittens.

Jimmy jabbers on and on to Casey. "Then the third one was born and—"

"Casey doesn't care, Jimmy," I bark.

Jimmy's face turns as red as a radish. "Shut up, Lillie Mae."

"I've never heard so much giggling in all my life," Tift complains, tromping up the hill.

I turn around and holler at Tift. "You didn't have to come here, you know."

Ellie punches me in the arm. "Lillie Mae."

"Well, he didn't." Tift picks on me all time, and I get tired of hearing it. Sometimes I'm mean back.

"Lord, help us get to the barn before a fight breaks out," Jesse prays, making everyone laugh.

When I reach the barn, I peer under the loft. Squeals reach the barn roof, only this time, it's not the kittens. It's the girls.

The boys glance at the kittens, shrug, and run off to play baseball. The girls crouch in the hay and giggle and coo. Nestled against Boots are two gray boys, one solid, and the other with white stripes, and two girls, both with black and white markings.

"I want one," Mary Olivia squeals.

"Me too," Sarah replies.

"Me three." Casey grins ear to ear.

I stare at the black one with a white chest and white paws. She looks the most like Boots. "Have you ever had a cat, Casey?"

She shakes her head. "No."

Mary Olivia looks up from the kittens. "A dog?"

"No."

Mary Olivia looks at her like she's crazy. "Why not?"

Casey hesitates. "Um. I just haven't."

Although she doesn't offer any information, I suspect I know the reason. What the other girls don't know yet is that Casey Culver is sick.

Chapter 13 ✦ Secrets

Secrets are hard to keep when they bottle up inside you. I'm like a Coca-Cola that's been shaken—pop the top, and I'll explode. I need to get Casey's secret off my chest and tell the one person I trust—Ellie. We don't have any secrets between us. Well, we didn't until I got the dumb idea to work with Violet.

"Lillie Mae. Are you listening to me?" Daddy stares at me across the supper table. My mouth is closed around my fork, and I'm not sure how long I've been like this.

"No, sir. I was daydreaming," I say, through a mouthful of mashed potatoes.

George snickers, and a half-chewed chunk of carrot flies out of his mouth and lands near Grace's plate. Billy roars with laughter.

"Gross, George," Grace whines. "Pick it up."

George reaches to get the carrot and spills Grace's milk on the table. White liquid flows across the table to my plate.

"Oh, my goodness. Look what you've done," Mama fusses. She jumps up from the table and grabs a towel, mopping up the milk.

"Be more careful, son," Daddy barks before turning his attention back to me. "See, Ruth." He looks at Mama and shakes his finger at me. "They're distracted."

"I'm not the one who spilled milk," I reply.

"Lillie?" It's meant as a warning, and for once, I close my mouth. Mama places the wet towels in the sink then comes back to the table, placing her hand on Daddy's arm. "Ellie. Lillie. You've been so distracted by the kittens, you're getting behind on your chores. If you can't keep up, we'll have to cut out the friend time after school."

"No," I shriek louder than I meant to. "We'll go to the garden tonight. Won't we Ellie?" She glares at me as I elbow her. I need to talk to her without my brothers listening.

"I don't think tonight is necessary. It'll be dark soon." Daddy picks up his plate and sets it in the sink. "Tomorrow after school, though, I expect you to pick all the ripe corn, not just a few pieces. Ya hear me?"

"Yes, sir," I answer. He's referring to my hurried job the other day. "We'll start on it now, Daddy." I use the sweetest tone I can muster.

"He said tomorrow." Ellie's voice is tense. I glare at her, and she lets out an exaggerated sigh. "Fine. We'll do a little tonight."

I smile. Twins don't need words. They just need the right look. Once the dishes are in the dishwasher and the table is clean, Ellie and I head to the garden.

Ellie puts both hands on her hips. "Okay, spill it. Why are we really here?"

I take in a deep breath. "Casey shared something with me the other day, and the secret is killing me."

Ellie shakes her head and pulls an ear of corn from a large stalk. "Why anyone shares a secret with you is beyond me. You always end up telling me."

"I know. But it's serious, Ellie." I pause, then look her in the eye. "Casey is sick."

Ellie lifts one eyebrow. "Sick as in she'll get better in a day or two?"

I shake my head back and forth. "No. She has leukemia. It means cancer."

Ellie drops the ear of corn on the ground. "I know what leukemia is, Lillie." Her voice quivers. "Is that why she moved here?"

"Sort of." I reach up, pull an ear of corn from a tall stalk, and drop it in the basket. "Her daddy had a job offer to move out of the city. They chose Triple Gap to give Casey a fresh start."

Ellie nods her head. "Poor Casey. That must be awful."

"That's not even half of it." I sigh and grab another ear from the same tall stalk. "I did something horrible." Tears fill the corners of my eyes as I tell Ellie about approaching Violet.

"Lillie! How could you do that?" Ellie shouts, throwing corn in the basket.

My tears spill onto my cheeks. "I know it was stupid. I was mad because she stole my best friend."

Ellie plops to the ground. "I told you your plan for getting your best friend back was a rotten idea. I can't believe you brought Violet into this."

I wipe my cheek with the back of my hand and sink down into the soil next to her. "I told Violet I didn't want to be a part of this anymore," I cry, desperately wanting Ellie to understand. "But she wasn't exactly cooperative."

Ellie scrunches her brows together. "What do you mean?"

"She said it was my idea in the first place, so whatever happens is my fault."

Ellie stares me in the eye. "Do you think Violet will tell anyone?"

Hanging my head, a tear falls to the basket. "I don't know."

Chapter 14   Running for Office

When the dismissal bell rings, I head to my locker to get my social studies homework. Slamming it shut, I meander toward the bus when Scully shouts my name.

"Wait up, Lillie Mae."

I glance over my shoulder and keep walking. I don't want to miss the bus.

Scully taps me on the shoulder. "Guess what?" He doesn't wait for me to answer. "I'm running for class president." A huge smile fills his face, showing all his teeth.

I stop and stare at him. "Where did that come from?"

He frowns. "I thought you'd be happy for me. Especially since I'll run against Violet." He pauses when I don't say anything. "It's a good way for me to get to know the kids around here."

"Oh, okay," I say.

"Wyatt's my campaign manager, and we need someone to introduce us around. You'd be perfect for the job since you know everyone."

He's right. Since I've lived in Triple Gap my whole life, I know almost everyone. Plus, most kids come from farming families like me, and we stick together. But, the news fills me with dread. I can't do anything to make Violet mad at me right now.

"I don't think that's a good idea," I mumble, continuing to walk toward the bus.

Scully tugs at my arm, making me stop in front of the exit. "Which part? Me running for president or you helping me?"

"Me helping."

"Oh." He shuffles his feet on the floor. "Well, I thought it would be, you know, fun to spend time together." His face turns red, and I realize what he's really trying to say.

Ellie was right. Scully has a crush on me. Embarrassed, I look away. "All right," my voice crackles. "I guess I could."

"Geez. Don't act so excited." He turns his back and starts to walk away.

Now I feel bad and grab his arm before he can get away. "Sorry, Scully. I'm tryin' not to make Violet mad at me right now."

"Why? What happened?"

"It's complicated." I should tell him the truth, but I can't. He'd hate me. "I'll help you, if you really need it."

He doesn't answer at first. Then, his face returns to his usual grin. "Great, thanks. See you tomorrow."

Could things get any worse?

The next morning, I take Scully around school and introduce him to as many kids as I can. At the end of third period, when I spot Betsy, I drag Scully over to meet her. "Hey, Betsy. Have you met Scully? He's running for class president."

Betsy's blonde hair flies in her face as she whips her head around. Her eyes go wide. "You're running against Violet Holt?" Her face fills with a wide-toothed grin.

"You bet." Scully winks at Betsy. "The first thing I will do as your class president is get better food in the school cafeteria."

Betsy's green eyes match the poster behind her. "Then you have my vote."

Scully shoves his gigantic camera into my gut. "Here, Lillie. Take a picture for the yearbook of me campaigning."

"That's your job," I say, fumbling with the camera.

"I can't exactly take a picture of myself, now can I? Press the big silver button on the top." He points to it, then steps back against the gray cinder block wall. Whipping his arm around Betsy, he pulls her into the picture. She grins and giggles.

I snap the picture, and Betsy flies to my side. "Since when are you interested in student council?"

"I'm not. I mean, I'm helping Scully today is all." My face heats up.

"You mean you're helping him win against Violet."

"Shh," I whisper in her ear. "Yeah, but I don't want Violet to know."

Betsy scrunches her eyebrows together. "Why?"

"It's complicated," I say for the second time.

Betsy frowns. "Well, I wanna help."

"Really?" My eyes go wide. Things may be looking up.

"What can I do?" she asks.

"Can you make posters and hang them around school tomorrow?"

"Sure." Betsy prances down the hall. "See you soon."

I turn to Scully. "It won't be hard to get the girls on your side. Girls like you," I say, nodding toward Betsy. "Your challenge is fighting Violet's daddy. Have you met Duke Holt?"

Scully shakes his head. "No. What's he got to do with what goes on at school?"

"Everything, considering he owns the town." I roll my eyes. "He controls the bank, so that controls the farmers. I don't think he's gonna take too kindly to a stranger in town competing with his daughter."

Scully scrunches his nose. "Small towns are weird."

I nod my head. "You have no idea."

By the time school dismisses, Scully's met almost all the kids at school. Jimmy led him around the cafeteria and introduced him to the boys on the baseball team. It helps to have a brother who knows the athletes. Jesse introduced him to the church kids. If I know Jesse, he's probably praying for a miracle so Scully can win. That boy sure knows how to pray.

When the dismissal bell rings, I pull my math book out of my locker. Ellie waits next to me as Scully rushes over.

"Thanks for helping today." Scully says. He stands there like I'm supposed to say something, until Ellie nudges me.

"Oh, uh, you're welcome," I answer. I step onto the school bus and plop down in the seat next to Ellie.

"Why were you embarrassed?" Ellie stares at me.

I love having a twin who understands what I'm feeling without me having to say a word. "You were right. Scully has a crush on me." I let out a loud groan.

Her eyes twinkle. "I know. I'm always right about these kinds of things."

"What am I supposed to do? I like Wyatt."

"Wyatt likes you too. What are you doing to make all the boys like you?"

"Nothing," I shriek, a little too loud.

Tift Johnson turns around in the seat in front of me. I glance at Ellie and slide my fingers across my lips like a zipper. No matter what, I don't want Tift to hear our conversation. I don't need any excuse for him to make fun of me. When Tift faces forward and babbles about baseball, I breathe a sigh of relief.

"I don't dress up. I don't fix my hair. I'm not even that nice." I look down at my lap, expecting Ellie to agree with me. "I don't know what's happening."

"I do." Ellie says, then looks out the window.

"Well, for Pete's sake." That's what Daddy always says when he's exasperated. "Don't leave me hangin'."

"You're being your Sour Lemon self." Ellie giggles.

"Huh?"

She throws her hands in the air. "You're being you, and that's what they like. You're real. You don't try to be fake or put on a show. You're just...you."

Chapter 15 Campaigning

After completing our chores and checking on the kittens, Ellie and I get to work on Scully's campaign. Before long, our kitchen is full of volunteers. The way I see it, if I get a lot of people to help, Violet won't know I was involved and she can't get mad at me. Casey, Mary Olivia, and Sarah cut out strips of paper, and Ellie and I write "Scully Jackson for Class President" in bold letters. Grace pours sweet tea in glasses for all the volunteers.

When I finish my last poster, my fingers curl in place around the marker. "I think Scully might be able to beat Violet with all this help."

"Maybe," Sarah says. "If Violet doesn't cheat."

"How can she cheat?" Casey asks.

"I wouldn't put anything past that girl." Sarah crumples the scraps of paper and drops them in the trash.

Mary Olivia stands up and stretches. "All Violet has to do is whine to her daddy, and Duke gives her whatever she wants."

I put my hands on my hips. "We gotta make sure that doesn't happen."

"Who wants to go see the kittens?" Ellie says. Squeals fill the room as we march out the door and head to the barn.

When Mary Olivia sees the kittens, she gasps. "They've grown so much."

"They're one week old," Grace announces. "Y'all can't hold them yet."

Ellie puts her hand on Grace's shoulder. "Grace thinks they're *her* babies."

"They are, Ellie," Grace snaps.

I fluff the blanket under Boots. "Mama says we can hold them when they're about two weeks old."

Casey gets a funny expression on her face. "I asked my parents if I could have one."

"And?" I raise one eyebrow.

"They didn't really answer. They said they'd think about it." Her face turns to a frown.

"Casey. I need to tell you somethin'." I stand up and shuffle my feet around the dirt floor, causing dust to fly.

Casey squats down near Boots and reaches in to pet her. Boots purrs and moves closer. "Okay."

"Um. Well, it's like this. I've done somethin'." I swallow hard.

Casey stands up and puts her arm around my shoulder. "You can tell me, you know."

"Hey, what's goin' on? You all right, Lillie?" Mary Olivia stands next to Sarah and Ellie stares at me from the ground.

With everyone watching, I get nervous. I need to be honest with Casey, but my mouth goes dry, and I can't get the words out. "I just wanted to say...that I hope your parents let you have a kitten."

Casey tilts her head to the side. "Oh. Thanks. I guess."

Mad at myself for chickening out, I run out of the barn.

When I arrive at school the next day, Betsy is true to her promise. Lining the main hallway are posters announcing Scully for president. I find her standing on a chair hanging the last poster.

"Wow. You're fast," I say.

She glances over her shoulder. "Had to get the word out quickly. Speeches are a week and a half away."

"Maybe you should have my job."

"No way, Lillie. There's no one better to introduce Scully around school. Between you and your brothers, y'all know everyone." Betsy slams her fist on the wall, securing the last of the tape. "Besides, a little birdie told me about a certain crush." She giggles and steps off the chair.

"Ellie told you?"

"I'll never tell." She smiles. "Scully's cute. And he's charming. Did you see him wink at me the other day?"

I giggle. "He does have a way with girls. And he's cute, I guess, if you like boys from New York."

"Not your type?" Betsy asks. I shake my head. "Ah, I get it. You still like Wyatt."

"Yep. Scully's nice and all. It's just weird since I like his cousin."

"Look at you. Two boys like you. If only Jess—" Betsy turns away and fiddles with the tape in her hand.

My eyes go wide. "Wait. You like my brother?"

"Don't tell him, please," Betsy begs. I'm too shocked to answer. "Lillie. Please don't say anything. I don't think he knows I exist."

My mind swirls trying to make sense of what's happening to all of us. When I finally settle on what Betsy said, I take a deep breath.

"Well, I gotta tell you. You picked a good one. It doesn't get much better than Jesse." I put my arm around Betsy and narrow my eyes. "Thank goodness you don't like Jimmy."

Chapter 16 Spying Again

When the school bus drops us off at the end of our long dirt driveway, I wave at Pappy standing on his front porch. "Y'all have a good day at school?"

"Yes, sir," Jesse answers.

"Learn anything?" Pappy asks.

"No, sir." I shake my head back and forth, making my braids fling in my face.

Pappy chuckles. "Guess y'all ought to try learning somethin' tomorrow." He always says the same thing, and I always laugh.

"We'll try harder tomorrow, Pappy," Jimmy hollers, laughing.

I stop to give Pappy a quick hug. "Daddy says I have to pick corn before I can go see the kittens." I groan and step off the porch.

"Sounds 'bout right to me," he hollers, winking at me. "Chores come first."

I run down the driveway, across the baseball diamond, and into the house. I leave my textbooks in my room and call for Mama. No answer.

"Where's Mama?" I ask Jesse as he heads to his room across the hall.

Jesse shrugs. "Saw Daddy up next to the hen houses. Check up there."

"Thanks," I say, and run up the hill. Mama throws feed to the hens in E house. I sneak up behind her. "Boo."

She whips her body around. "Hi, Lillie. You heading to the garden?"

"Yes, ma'am," I say.

Daddy sticks his head around the corner. "I need you and Ellie to finish those rows on the west side today."

"Yes, sir." I have no idea which part of our garden is west. With my luck, I'd pick the wrong side, so I wait next to the chicken houses for Ellie. Mama's high-pitched squeal makes my ears perk up, and I inch closer to listen.

"That's good news, right?" Mama asks.

"Yep. Coach said Jimmy will definitely make the team," Daddy answers.

"Honey, that's wonderful. Have you told Jimmy yet?"

"No way. Don't want his grades to slip again. Ever since that girl came into his life, he suddenly cares about school."

"Casey," Mama corrects. "Her name is Casey."

"Yep. That's the one. You think she likes Jimmy back?" Daddy asks.

I scrunch up my nose and shake my head even though no one can see me.

Mama giggles like a schoolgirl. "I don't think so. Casey's a nice girl who needed a friend. Lillie Mae has been a good friend to her since she moved here."

I hang my head. *If Mama only knew.*

"Is that right?" Daddy doesn't sound convinced. He has a way of knowing when I've gotten myself into a tangled mess.

Before Mama can respond, I bolt for the garden. Ellie bends down in the thick of a cornstalk. When she hears me, she glances up. "What did they say?"

"Who? What?" I respond.

Ellie rolls her eyes. "You can't play that game with me. I know you were spyin' on Mama and Daddy."

I blink my eyes and tilt my head to one side. "Who, me?"

"Oh, please," Ellie barks. "Are you gonna tell me or not?"

I make sure no one else is listening, then I lean in real close. "Jimmy's on the team."

"Really?" Ellie smiles.

"Yep. Daddy hasn't told him yet, so don't tell anyone. Coach said his grades will be good enough to make it."

"Jimmy will be so happy."

"All because of Casey." I look away.

Ellie frowns. "You should be happy for him."

"I am. It's not that. It's..." I take a deep breath. "Mama said I've been a good friend to Casey. She's wrong, you know. I'm not a good friend."

Ellie lets out a loud sigh. "You can be. You've just made some bad choices."

My mouth twists up and I grumble under my breath. "You sound like Mama."

By the time Ellie and I strip the cornstalks in what we hope is the west side of the field, Casey's mom pulls in the driveway. Sarah is the first to make it up the hill to the barn, with Mary Olivia and Casey on her heels. The kittens nuzzle against Boots, all trying to get milk.

I reach in and pull out the black kitten with a white chest and white paws. Handing her to Casey, the kitten purrs. "Mama finally let us hold them this morning for the first time."

Casey nestles the kitten against her chest. "She's precious."

"Grace thinks so too." Ellie laughs. "She held each one like a baby doll, purring and cooing right along with them."

"I can see why," Casey says. "You're a sweet baby, aren't you?"

Ellie hands the gray kitten with white stripes to Sarah and gives Mary Olivia the solid gray boy.

"I wanna take this little guy home with me," Sarah coos. "Mary Olivia, let's ask Mama if we can have him."

Mary Olivia beams. "Or this guy. He's super soft." She rubs the gray fur against her face. "This is so much fun, all of us hanging around together. We should go shopping this weekend." Mary Olivia sets the gray kitten near Boots. "Do you think your mom would take us, Casey?"

"Probably. She loves shopping. I'll ask her."

Sunlight streams inside as the barn door opens.

"Ask me what?" Mrs. Culver steps inside.

Casey jumps up, and grabs her by the arm. "Mom. Come meet Boots and her kitties."

Mrs. Culver is dressed to the hilt, in high-heeled black pumps with black bell-bottom pants and a red blouse. She doesn't look like she belongs on a farm. I expect her to gasp and pull away from the smelly barn and dirty cats. Instead, she sits in the hay and listens to Casey babble about wanting a kitten.

"That one is my favorite. See her white chest? She looks like Daddy when he wears a Tuxedo." Casey turns to her mom. "I'm going to call her Tux."

"We'll have to see about a cat. I'm not sure if they are clean enough..." Mrs. Culver's face turns as red as the tomatoes in our garden. "I didn't mean that the way it sounded, Ruth," she says to Mama. "I apologize. It's just that Casey is—"

"Wanting to go shopping, tomorrow. Aren't you Casey?" I stare at her until she answers.

"Oh, yeah. Right." Casey turns toward me and mouths, "Thank you."

Mrs. Culver smiles. "I'm happy to take the girls shopping on Saturday. If that's all right with you, Ruth. And of course we'll also have to check with Mrs. Montgomery."

"Our Mama will say yes as long as we have our chores done," Mary Olivia adds.

"Same thing goes here, girls," Mama answers. "You're welcome to go once you've finished your chores."

Mrs. Culver smiles. "All right then. Saturday it is."

Chapter 17 Uncle Chicken

Before I can go shopping with my friends, my family piles into our Chevy truck and heads to The Mill, like we do every Saturday. I don't mind because it's the one time I get to see Uncle Chicken. I've got a good math problem worked up for him. As we get close, I'm more excited than ever about trying to stump him. Before Daddy puts the truck in park, I hop over the tailgate and leap out of the bed.

"Here, Billy. Grab this pole," Jesse hollers behind me. My brothers love fishing for trout in the stream below the building.

I run inside and find Uncle Chicken surrounded by adults. He sees me and grins, showing all his gums. "Well, if it ain't the old twin."

Here we go with our regular exchange. "I'm not old yet, Uncle Chicken."

He throws his head back as if that's the first time he's heard that one. "I gotta finish up with these folks, but I wanna hear whatcha got fur me today." He shouts over his shoulder. "Henry? We need some seed up here."

I grin. "Okay. I'll come back in a few minutes. Oh, and Daddy needs straw and feed."

"Henry? Ya got that? Straw and feed for the Liles."

"Yep. Got it, Chicken," Henry answers from somewhere in The Mill.

Uncle Chicken chuckles. "See ya 'round, kiddo."

"See ya," I say.

Strolling out of the building, I head down the hill to see who's here today. Mary Olivia waves me over. I bound toward her. "We're still going shoppin' today, right?" I bob my eyebrows up and down.

"Of course. Where do you wanna go?" Mary Olivia asks.

I smile. "I wanna take Ellie to Lennard's. She's never been there."

"I was thinkin' the same thing." Mary Olivia giggles. "Sarah's never been there either."

"I hope that's okay with Mrs. Culver," I say.

"Me too. Hey, wanna put our feet in the water?"

"Sure." I shriek when the icy cold water hits my toes. My brothers wade in the creek up to their ankles, casting one fishing pole after another. The cold doesn't seem to stop them.

"I got one!" George shouts. He looks around to see who's paying attention. He sees me, and holds up a trout the size of my hand.

I give him a thumbs up. "Good one," I laugh.

George grins ear to ear, proud of his catch. Billy takes it off the hook and hands it to George who tries to throw it back into the stream. Only, he slings it backward, and it lands on my foot. Shrieking, I plunge into the freezing shallow water. Everyone chuckles at the girl attacked by the three-inch trout. George laughs so hard he can't catch his breath. Mary Olivia offers me her hand and pulls me up. At least Mary Olivia has the decency to ask if I'm all right.

"Yeah, I'm fine. No thanks to you, George," I yell.

Ellie stands on the shore behind me with Sarah, the two of them cracking up. "Aw, don't be too hard on him. He was tryin' to show you his prize catch."

Billy throws his arm around George's shoulder. "Now *that* was a good one!"

I scowl at Billy. "I'm freezing. I'm going inside."

"I'll go with you," Mary Olivia offers. "You gonna try to stump Uncle Chicken today?"

"You bet."

When we reach the top of the hill, Mama frowns. "Lillie Mae. What on Earth happened to you?"

Before I can answer, Mary Olivia chimes in. "She got attacked by a killer trout." This sends Mary Olivia into hysterics as she laughs at her own joke.

I don't find it near as funny. "George released his fish my way. When it hit my toe, I freaked out and fell backward."

"Ah." Mama winks at Mary Olivia. "Lillie doesn't like anything touching her feet. Fish or snakes."

"Snakes?" Mary Olivia looks from me to Mama.

I moan. "There was a snake last summer in our garden that scared me half to death." I shudder at the memory of that black snake attacking me. "Come on. Let's go see Uncle Chicken."

When I step inside, stares from the adults fill the room. I don't bother to explain why my pants are dripping wet in the middle of October. I spot Uncle Chicken loading seed on a forklift and sneak up behind him.

"You ready for this, Uncle Chicken? I've got a good one today," I announce.

He spins around and chuckles. "Yep. Whatcha got fur me?"

"What is fifty-five thousand, five hundred and fifty-five times forty-four thousand, four hundred and forty-four?"

I take a deep breath, awaiting his answer. He turns his head to the side, rubs his gums together, and places his hand on his chin like he's thinking hard.

"Two billion, four hundred sixty-nine million, eighty-six thousand, four hundred and twenty."

Before I can say wow, the crowd erupts in applause. No one knows for sure how Uncle Chicken does it. I've always wondered why such a smart man never went to college. One day, I'll have to ask him. Mary Olivia whoops and hollers before sauntering back outside.

Uncle Chicken rests his hand on my shoulder. "Ya know the secret, right?"

"Yes, sir. Stay in school," I say.

He chuckles. "Yep. That's it."

Before he can say the next part, I volunteer the information. "And I promise I will."

"Atta girl." He squeezes my shoulder, then goes back to loading heavy bags of seed onto the forklift. Without turning around, he asks, "What did ya ever decide about the Culver family?"

"I like them. Me and Casey are friends now. I'm going shopping with her later today."

He glances over his shoulder. "Hopefully not like that?"

"No." I laugh, shaking my wet hair in my face. "I'll put dry clothes on first."

He grins, showing his toothless gums. "Ya stayin' out of trouble?"

I swallow hard. "Tryin' to."

"Uh, huh. That's good. That's real good." He pauses and runs his fingers through what's left of his hair. I can tell he wants to say something else. "Ya know why the Culvers moved to Triple Gap?"

"Yeah. Her daddy got the job building the bridge across the lake," I reply.

"Yep. That upset a few local folks 'round here. Ya ever hear folks talkin' bad about them?"

"Nope."

He nods. "That's good. If you do, don't pay it no mind."

"Yes, sir," I reply, not understanding where this is going.

Sensing my confusion, he continues. "Rumors can be hurtful."

He stares into my soul. I can't breathe. Ashamed, I want to run away. I tilt my head sideways and narrow my eyes, my detective skills in full alert. "Is there something you're not tellin' me?" I fully expect him to tell me that he knows all about Violet and my evil plot to get rid of Casey.

He scratches his head. "Everyone at some point's gotta own up to their mistakes."

I scrunch my brows together. "Huh?"

He chuckles his silent laugh. "Ya stay away from trouble now, ya hear?" He turns toward the back of the building, and shouts at Henry. "You got that hay loaded yet?"

What's he's not telling me?

Chapter 18 The Real Daisy

When Ellie and I arrive at the Culver's, Mary Olivia and Sarah sit on Casey's bed, glancing through a fashion magazine. The models wear bell-bottom pants with short tops revealing their stomachs.

"I wish my Mama would let me wear a top like that." Sarah points to the red and white checkered shirt tied in the front.

"That looks like what Daisy Duke would wear." I giggle.

Mary Olivia gasps. "Oh, Casey. Did we ever tell you that everyone thought you were Daisy Duke when you first came to Triple Gap?"

I roll my eyes. "Not everyone."

Mary Olivia lets out a loud puff of air. "Well, I did."

Casey laughs. "Are you serious? You thought I was the real Daisy Duke?"

"Yep." Mary Olivia scrunches her nose. "Sounds pretty stupid, now that I think about it." Everyone giggles. "Violet was so jealous of you, she couldn't see straight."

"Yeah, I figured that out real quick." Casey slips on a dark-blue jacket.

"Come to think of it, Lillie was jealous of you too." Mary Olivia stares at me. "Weren't you, Lillie?" Four sets of eyes bore into me as the laughter stops.

"Jealous? Why?" Casey questions.

"Um, um," I stutter. "I think there's something you should know." Casey stands in front of her dresser, waiting for me to continue. I swallow. "Well, you see—"

"Have y'all ever read *Little Women*?" Ellie interrupts.

Sweet Tea Ellie just saved my life.

"I read it last year," Sarah answers. "I loved Jo. She was so brave."

I must not be like Jo after all.

Ellie smiles. "Jo is a good character, but I like Beth."

Sarah giggles. "That's because she's sweet, like you."

Ellie puts her arm around me. "And because her best friend is Jo." I grin bigger than Meemaw's biscuits on Sunday morning.

"My mom and I read that book together," Casey says just above a whisper. Her face droops, and the smile that normally fills her face vanishes. She turns to Ellie. "Do you know what happens to Beth?"

Ellie shakes her head. "No, what?"

Sarah taps Casey on the arm. "Maybe we should let it be a surprise for Ellie. Besides, I thought we were going shopping?"

"Yeah. Let's go." Mary Olivia jumps up and throws the magazine onto Casey's bed. "Y'all can talk about old books later."

Ellie stomps her feet. "It's called a classic."

When we reach Lennard's, I hold Ellie's hand. "Close your eyes." I open the door and whisper, "Now open."

Ellie gasps, and her jaw drops. She stares at the crystal chandelier hanging in the entry, its light reflecting little stars on the walls. I follow her gaze to the sparkles on white cloth hangers, each outfit separated by color.

"It's beautiful," she whispers.

I grin. "I told you. It's like being in heaven."

We stroll through the store as Mrs. Culver takes Casey to see a dress in the back. Ellie touches a yellow silk fabric, rubbing it against her cheek. I show Ellie the outfit I tried on last time.

"You put this on?" She holds the white bell-bottom pants and fiddles with the price tag hanging from the gold blouse. "Did you look at the price?"

"Um hum." I giggle. "I felt like a princess. Do you wanna try something on? You and Sarah could model for us this time."

Ellie's smile gets even bigger. "If it's all right with Mrs. Culver."

"Let's go ask."

Once we have permission, Ellie and Sarah select expensive outfits and step into the dressing room. When they come out to model, I jump out of my cushioned white chair and spin Ellie around and around.

"I love it!" When Casey comes out of the dressing room modeling a simple black dress, I gasp. "Casey, you look really pretty."

"Lillie needs to wear a dress like that for Scully's speech." Ellie's eyebrows bob up and down.

"Why would she dress up for that?" Casey asks.

"Because." Ellie shrugs. "Scully's got a crush on her bigger than the Mississippi River."

"Ellie," I shriek, punching her in the arm.

"You and Scully?" Mary Olivia's eyes go wide.

"No. I don't like him," I insist. "He's just a friend."

Ellie continues to tease me. "He doesn't think so."

"I think he's cute," Sarah says.

"You think all the boys are cute," Mary Olivia barks at her sister.

Sarah's face fills with a mischievous smile. "What's wrong with that?"

I roll my eyes. "I don't like Scully, okay? So stop it."

Sarah points to Ellie. "She started it."

"Ugh. I need to get out of here," I groan. All this talk of boys and dressing up has me breaking out in hives.

Chapter 19 ● Speechless

Scully stands at his locker fiddling with the combination. He bangs on the metal, creating echoes down the hall. I sneak up behind him and shout, "Scully Scrub. You still havin' trouble opening your locker?"

He spins around so fast, he reminds me of the weather vane on top of our barn roof. "No."

With less than a week left before the big election, he's wound tighter than a lasso around a bull's horns. When his locker pops open on the third try, he lets out a whoop.

"Try slowin' down," I say. "You live in the South now. We move at the pace of snapping turtles 'round here."

Scully shakes his head. "Where do you come up with this stuff?"

I shove my shoulders up and throw my hands in the air. Pulling out my social studies book, I slam my locker and walk to class.

"Hey, Lillie," Scully calls after me. I turn around. "I wanted to tell you...well...thanks for helping with all this election stuff. No matter what happens on Wednesday, I've had fun getting to know you." He shuffles his feet on the tile floor and sticks his hands in his pockets. "I see why Wyatt likes you."

"He does?" My eyes go wide. Embarrassed at my reaction, I start to sweat. "I mean, cool."

Scully laughs. "Nice try. I know you like him too."

"You do?" I say sheepishly, wondering who told him. "I'm sorry, Scully." And I meant it.

He puts his chin in the air. "It's cool. Really. It's just that, well, you were the first person, other than Wyatt, to pay any attention to me."

I sigh. "If it's not too weird, I'd like us to still be friends. You're one of the coolest guys I know."

He beams and flashes his famous smile. "Friends it is. Now come on before you make me late to class."

We get two steps down the hall when Violet stops Scully in his tracks. She stands in front of him with both hands on her hips, blocking us from going any further. "Hello, Scrub. How nice that Lillie Mae decided to help you run against me."

"I didn't help," I bark. "If Scully wins, it's because he's nice to people. Maybe you ought to try that sometime."

Scully smiles at me. "Thanks, Lillie, but you helped a lot."

"No-I-didn't." My teeth clench together, and my voice grows louder. "Good luck to both of you."

I charge down the hall before he can say anything else. When I turn around, Scully stands with his mouth open. I take a step backward and crash into Casey and Mary Olivia.

"Shoo. That was a close one. I think Violet believed me, but I feel bad not explaining to Scully what's going on." Mary Olivia and Casey aren't paying a bit of attention to what I'm saying. "Casey? What's wrong?"

Casey's face drains of all color as tears spill onto her cheeks. "How could you, Lillie Mae?"

"How could I what?" I ask.

"Tell everyone about me."

My eyes go wide. "Casey, I don't know what you're talking about."

Casey's eyes are red and puffy. "You told everyone I'm contagious."

Mary Olivia stares at me like I'm a stranger. "And that she failed out of private school."

I feel like I'm going to be sick. "I didn't tell anyone. I swear."

Casey brushes her tears with the back of her hand. "I trusted you, Lillie. I thought you were my friend."

"I am your friend." I grab her hand, but she yanks it away.

"Not anymore." Casey runs down the hall toward the exit.

"You're not my friend anymore either, Lillie." Mary Olivia shakes her head. "I can't believe you would do that."

She flees after Casey, leaving me standing alone, speechless.

My blood boils and I stomp toward Violet. A group of girls near the lunchroom surround her. The rumor about Casey spread faster than the flu virus.

"She's contagious?" one girl gasps.

"Do you think I have it?" another asks.

"I think I caught it," a frail-looking girl whines. "I gotta go home." She shivers like she has a fever.

Barging in, I grab Violet's arm and yank her away from the others. "How dare you! I told you that in confidence, so you'd know why I didn't want to be part of your stupid plan."

Violet smirks. "It was *your* plan. Remember, Lillie? You're the one who came to me for help."

"Not so you could do this!" I scream.

Violet puts her hands on her hips. "*You* said you wanted to get rid of Casey. I helped you out. See those girls?" She points to the group. "They came right back to me."

"They're not your friends. They do what you say so you won't talk about them behind their back. That's not friendship."

Violet smirks like the Grinch. "It will help me win the election, though."

I shake my head. "You're even more of a bully than I thought." I race for the bathroom and lose my lunch.

When Scully and Wyatt spot me coming out of the bathroom, they both look away as if I'm not there. Tears burn my eyes. Wyatt takes a few steps then turns around, glaring at me. "Is it true? Did you really start those rumors about Casey?"

I place my head in my hands and scream. "No! How could you think I would do something like that?"

When I raise my head, Wyatt's scrunches his eyes together. "I didn't think so. That's not the Lillie Mae I met last summer who would do anything to save her family's farm. I had to be sure."

Scully grabs me by the arm. "Come on. We've got work to do if we're going to win an election."

Chapter 20 Taking Responsibility

This day moves slower than an opossum crossing the highway. Whispers of Casey's unknown disease spread like a virus through the school building. The bigger the rumors grow, the more hateful the kids become toward me. I wonder why no one, except Wyatt and Scully, bothered to ask me if any of this is true.

When I finally get home, I'm too exhausted to climb the ladder to my bunk bed, so I collapse on Ellie's bottom bunk, wetting her pillow with my tears. Mama comes in and shuts the door.

She sits next to me and stays silent for a few seconds. "I got a call from Mrs. Culver today." A small whimper escapes my lips. "Casey will no longer be working with Jimmy on his studies. Do you know what that means?" Mama doesn't wait for me to answer. "It means, if Jimmy's grades fall again, he won't make the baseball team."

"I thought he was already on the team?" My voice crackles through the tears.

Thank goodness Daddy told Jimmy the other night, and Jimmy told all of us. Otherwise, I'd have to explain how I know without revealing I was spying on her conversation with Daddy.

"As long as his grades remain good between now and then." Mama sighs. "Lillie Mae, your decisions affect others in this family. I'm very disappointed in you."

"I didn't do anything wrong. Why is everyone so mad at me?"

Mama gives me a sad smile. "Were you angry at Casey when you approached Violet?"

"Yeah, because I thought she stole my best friend. But none of this is my fault. Violet spread those rumors, not me."

Mama grits her teeth. "You're right. Violet was wrong. But you need to take responsibility for your part. You came up with a plan to trick Casey into moving away. That's a form of bullying, Lillie, and we do not tolerate bullying in our family." Mama sighs again. "Your father and I have never *made* you be friends with anyone, but we expect you to be kind to everyone."

"I didn't mean for any of this to happen." My voice gets choked by my sobs.

"I know you didn't mean it, but there are always consequences for our actions. That's why it's so important to make wise choices."

My voice is loud and desperate. "I tried telling Violet to drop the whole idea because Casey's sick. I told her I didn't want to be a part of this anymore."

"Lillie Mae. Sit up and look at me." It's not up for discussion. I sit up and wipe my cheeks with my hands, unable to look Mama in the eye. "Look at me," she says again. "Casey told you about her leukemia in confidence. You violated her trust. It wasn't your place to tell Violet."

"I was *trying* to explain to Violet why I wouldn't help her." My voice is forceful but I feel afraid. I shiver as a tear falls down my cheek and lands on my lap. "Casey and Mary Olivia will never wanna be friends with me again."

Mama pushes my long, brown hair off my face. "They may not. That's a consequence you will have to face. The first thing you must do is to take responsibility for your part."

My eyes move up to meet her gaze. "How do I do that? I don't know how to make this right."

She looks out my window. "I have someone you need to talk to."

Chapter 21 A Changed Man

Mama drags me out of the house without another word. At least I know when *not* to open my mouth. Climbing in our Chevy truck, I sit up front next to Mama. I turn on the radio, hoping for a happy song. Instead, the song, "Sad Eyes", fills the speakers. I turn off the radio.

A tear escapes from my eye, so I turn toward the window feeling confused. I stare out the window and watch as my farm disappears from view. Farms on both sides of the road will soon be shopping centers. The pig farm on the way to The Mill has a giant sign out front that reads, "Pumpkins for Sale."

There's something sad about watching your town change. I imagine by the time I'm Mama's age, there won't be many farms left. Seems like everyone wants development. I thought I did too. Now, all I want is for things to go back to the way they used to be, before new people moved to town and shopping malls were built. Back to a simpler time when all I needed was my farm and my baseball field.

As Mama turns onto Main Street, I wipe the tear that made its way down to my cheek. The square is lined with scarecrows resting on hay bales, holding bright orange pumpkins. When Mama parks in front of Sawnee Community Bank, my mouth goes dry.

"What are we doing here?" My voice catches in my throat.

Mama opens her door. "Come on, Lillie Mae. Let's go inside."

I open the truck door, step out into the cool October breeze, and walk inside the bank. I've been here dozens of times, but this time, a feeling a dread fills my heart. Surely Mama doesn't want me to talk to—

"Hello, Duke," Mama says, smiling.

I shrink and stare at my feet. *Duke Holt, Violet's father.*

"Ruth." Duke nods his head. "Y'all come on in my office."

My legs stick to the red carpet. Mama gives my back a gentle nudge, and I step inside a large office with glass doors. Mr. Holt motions for me to sit in a soft, brown leather chair across from a large desk with fancy wood paneling on the side. The chair is much bigger than me, and I feel small as I sink down into the cushion.

Mama and Mr. Holt stop in the doorway and whisper before Mama motions for me to follow her back out the door. "Lillie Mae. Let's go to the park across the street."

"Yes, ma'am." My voice shakes, still unsure of what I'm doing here.

I follow them out the door and across the street. I've been to this park dozens of times while Mama runs errands in the square. I make a beeline for my favorite spot next to the fountain and stick my hand in the cold water. It splashes onto my sleeve, making goose bumps run up and down my arms. Mr. Holt sits next to me on the concrete wall, and Mama takes a seat on the other side of me, resting her hand on my knee to steady the shaking.

Mr. Holt clears his throat. "Your mama tells me you need to hear a story about responsibility." I remain quiet, unsure what to say. "I think you know by now I wasn't the nicest man around. Some folks still think I'm not very nice." I glance at Mama, but she stares at Mr. Holt, nodding for him to continue. "Anyway, you know what happened with your daddy and me, right?"

"Yes, sir. You tried to steal our farm because of something Daddy did to you in high school."

"Yes, well *steal* is a strong word. My plan was to make your daddy pay for ruining my baseball career. I thought revenge would make me happy. All it did was cause more pain for those around me. I taught Violet to get her way at any cost, even if it means people get hurt along the way. But I was wrong. Nothing could be further from the truth, Lillie Mae. If you hurt people, you haven't won. You've lost everything that matters."

He touches his eye with the back of his hand. *Are those tears?* I sit frozen like the stone statue in the middle of the fountain.

"My hate cost me my business and my employees, and it nearly cost me my family," Duke continues. "Did you know my wife was on her way out the door last year with the kids?"

I want to say it doesn't surprise me and I wish Violet had left Triple Gap. Then, none of this would have happened. But instead, I whisper, "No, sir."

"Yep. She sure was, and quite frankly, I don't blame her. I was bitter, and Violet was becoming just like me."

She is like you. I don't dare look at him, wondering why in the world Mama thought coming here was a good idea.

After an awkward silence, Duke stands up and rubs his hands through his hair. "I know what Violet's done. The school called me."

I look up at him and see something I've never seen in his eyes. *Regret, perhaps?*

"They did?" My voice quivers.

He nods. "Yes. I'm afraid I've been a poor example to Violet. She's become a bully like me. You see, Lillie, not only did I have to apologize to your father, I had to make things right. I took full responsibility for my actions and stepped down as chairman of the bank."

Wait, I was just in his fancy office. Why do they still let him use it? Before I can ask, he volunteers the information.

"Sometimes, when we take responsibility for our actions, things work out. The bank asked me back, so here I am. But not everything worked out so well. I lost the building contracts to a man named Culver." He pauses and stares at me with his deep, blue eyes, making me shudder. "You know that name?"

My eyes go wide and the air leaks from my lungs. "Casey Culver's father?"

"Yep. That's the one." Mr. Holt shuffles his feet. "He got the contract for the shopping mall and the interstate bridge over the lake. It was a consequence I had to face when I took responsibility for deceiving your father."

So this is what Uncle Chicken knew. He was trying to tell me Duke took responsibility for his actions. Or I needed to take responsibility.

Duke looks at Mama, and she smiles. "I told the truth, Lillie Mae. I told everyone the truth about what I did to your daddy and to others like him. It was too late to get back some of the farms. I will always regret that."

He gazes in the distance, and I notice his eyes are moist again. This is not the same man I knew last summer—the man that nearly took my home away. I open my mouth to speak, and the words that come out surprise me.

"I'm really sorry for your loss, Mr. Holt."

He turns to face me and smiles for the first time. "Thank you. What is most important here is that I told the truth and owned up to what I'd done. I've explained all this to Violet. Now, you need to do the same. Own up to your part in this mess. Violet will take responsibility for the rest. You both need to tell the truth."

Swallowing hard, I choke on my words. "Okay. I will."

Mama puts her arm around me. "Thank you, Duke."

He nods his head. "You're welcome."

Mama and I stand up, and she squeezes my shoulders. We start to walk toward the car when I turn back around, staring at Mr. Holt. His once blazing blue eyes have softened and seem kinder.

"Mr. Holt? Do you think Violet will tell the truth? That she started those rumors about Casey, not me?"

Duke sighs. "She will. I will make sure of it."

Squishing my eyes together, I turn my head to one side. "How are you gonna do that?"

"I'm going to be there tomorrow during the speeches, that's how. Spreading rumors is bullying, Lillie Mae." He looks deep into my sad eyes. "Violet needs to know bullying, in any form, is wrong."

I give him a half-smile. My emotions are all over the place. "Okay. I'll see you tomorrow."

Chapter 22 Jesse

Mama and I don't say much on the way home. I keep thinking about what Mr. Holt told me, about how much he'd lost. *If I tell the truth, will I lose all my friends?* The thought rattles me. I need a way to make this right without telling everyone my part in the whole thing. Maybe I can blame Violet and let her take the fall. After all, she was the one who spread the rumors in the first place.

"Lillie Mae." Mama interrupts my thoughts. I turn from the window to face her. "Your father and I decided you can eat supper in your room tonight by yourself. It will give you a chance to figure out how to make things right."

This is the second time today Mama has referred to Daddy as *my father.* When Mama gets all formal it's a sure sign she is a-n-g-r-y.

Tears burn my eyes. "Can I at least go see the kittens, first?" I plead.

A slight smile fills her face. "All right. When we get home, you can peek in on them."

A tear falls onto my lap. "I'm sorry, Mama."

"I know you are, Lillie Mae. These are simply consequences for your mistake."

When we arrive home, I climb out of the truck. My brothers and sisters play outside, enjoying the cool October air.

I keep my head down so my brothers won't know I've been crying and run up the hill to the barn. Boots is nowhere to be found, but the kittens climb on top of each other in the corner. I reach into the pile and pull out Tux, the black and white kitten Casey named. I put her to my face, rubbing her soft fur against my cheek, and collapse on a hay bale.

"Hey, Tux. I bet you miss Casey, huh? She hasn't come to see you because of me." A tear lands on her black fur, and I do my best to dry her off. "I really messed up this time."

A shadow appears behind me. "Lil?"

"Yeah?" My voice crackles, and I wipe my cheek.

Jesse strolls over and sits down beside me. I continue to pet Tux, wondering what Jesse's doing here. He clears his throat.

"Remember when Casey first moved to town, and you thought she'd stolen your best friend?"

"Um hum," I say. "I did what you said. I prayed and asked God to give me back my best friend. Apparently, he doesn't listen."

"So you took control?" Jesse has a way of getting to the heart of the matter before I realize what he's done. Unsure of how to respond, I stay quiet. "Don't know if you remember or not, but I told you God answers our prayers in different ways. Sometimes he makes us wait for an answer, and you asked me why."

My mind swirls as I try to recall what he told me. "You said, there's something I'm supposed to be learnin'."

Jesse nods his head. "Yep. That's what you gotta figure out."

Chapter 23   The Speech

Wednesday has finally arrived—the day the candidates make their speeches. I'm more nervous than a turkey at Thanksgiving. Scully stands in front of my locker looking down at note cards, whispering what I assume is his speech. He's dressed up like he's going to church, in a navy blue suit with a red tie.

I reach for my locker as he steps to the side. "Is your speech ready?"

"Ready as ever." Scully shakes his arms, flailing them like a doll. He looks ridiculous. "I'm shaking off the jitters. That's a good Southern expression, right?"

I nod my head. "Yeah. But drop the accent. It's terrible."

He gives me a thumbs up. "Ready to go?"

I shuffle my feet. "Um. I'll meet you there in a minute."

He shrugs. "Okay."

"Scully? No matter what happens today, I just wanted to tell you...good luck."

He grins like he won the election. "Thanks."

Mrs. Davenport, the principal, transformed the gymnasium to an auditorium. A podium with a microphone stands in the center of the stage. Behind the podium are several brown metal cafeteria chairs. What was once the basketball court is now row after row of metal chairs.

I spot Mary Olivia sitting near the back. She glances in my direction then turns away. Casey hasn't returned to school, and

I wonder if she ever will. Ellie sits a few rows back from the front and waves me over. I squeeze in between her and Jesse.

Jesse leans over and whispers in my ear. "Ready?"

I give a slight nod.

Mrs. Davenport walks on stage and taps the microphone. The sound vibrating in the room makes everyone cover their ears. Coach Joe, who apparently runs the soundboard, leaps up and turns off the microphone. Mrs. Davenport's lips are moving, but no one can hear her. A few kids in the back start to giggle, and in a matter of seconds, the entire school body bursts into laughter.

"Test. Test." Mrs. Davenport screeches into the microphone as the sound blares across the gym. The murmurs grow louder. "All right, boys and girls. Let's settle down now." She waits until the snickering stops.

"Welcome to Peachtree Junior High's student council election. We will hear from each of our candidates. Scully Jackson will go first, followed by Violet Holt. In your next period class, you will receive a ballot in which you'll select the candidate of your choice for class president. Now, without further ado, please welcome our first speaker, Scully Jackson."

Mrs. Davenport sits in one of the metal chairs on stage as Scully steps to the microphone. He opens his mouth to speak—only nothing comes out. I mean, no words anyway. A spray of spit hits the microphone with such force that Jeffrey Trammell, sitting in the front row, flies out of his seat.

"Gross! He spit on me." Jeffrey stands helpless as the crowd roars with laughter and Coach Joe escorts Jeffrey out of the gym.

Poor Scully. His face has more spots than a leopard. Wyatt sits on the front row in a dark, three-piece suit and points to the notecards in Scully's hand. Scully looks down, then smiles at the crowd.

"Students at Peachtree Junior High, welcome," he shouts above the crowd. Mrs. Davenport stands on stage with one finger to her mouth and her other hand on her hip. After a few seconds, the kids are quiet.

"I'm Scully Jackson. I moved here this year from upstate New York, and I am proud to say I am now a true Southerner—I eat grits for breakfast, lunch, and dinner."

Cheers erupt in the gym, and Scully has everyone's attention. When he smiles, a group of girls in the front row giggle and point to him. Scully goes on to promise better food in the cafeteria and cleaner bathrooms.

"Thank you for your time and please vote Scully for President."

The kids applaud, mostly girls, and Scully sits down. I take in a deep breath as Mrs. Davenport announces the next speaker. Violet wears a pale yellow pantsuit. It looks like one I saw at Lennard's. In the silence, the gym door slams, and everyone turns around. Duke Holt walks to the front row and takes Jeffrey Trammell's seat.

My heart races faster than Uncle Chicken answers math problems. Violet introduces herself, but I can't hear what she's saying over the pounding in my chest. When Ellie reaches over and squeezes my hand, I look at the stage.

"And I promise to improve the stands next to our football field. We should have somewhere decent to sit while we watch our star athletes." She bats her eyelashes at the boys on the football team sitting together near the back of the room. A few boys whistle in approval. *That's one way to win their vote.* Someone in the crowd clears his throat. I glance at Duke.

"So, please vote Violet Holt for President. Oh, and before you do, you should know I started those rumors about Casey Culver."

Every head in the room pops up and stares at Violet Holt. She looks down at notecards propped up on the podium and begins to read.

"It was a mean thing to do. Casey is an outstanding member of our school and is one of the brightest students at Peachtree Junior High, and she did not fail out of private school. She is not, nor has she ever been, contagious. So please don't leave school today thinking that you have the virus. Instead, stay at school and vote Violet for President. Thank you very much."

A few kids politely applaud. Her gaggling girl following stands and cheers triumphantly. Ellie and I roll our eyes at the same time.

"Some apology," Ellie growls. "She forgot to say she was sorry."

I hang my head and tug at a hangnail on my cuticle. My stomach churns, and I feel like I'm about to throw up. "I don't think I can do this."

Jesse leans over. "You can do it, Lil. I prayed about it."

Good old Jesse. Once he prays about something, he believes God will answer. I wish I had that kind of faith.

As Violet sits down, Mrs. Davenport goes back to the microphone. "We have one more student that requested to say a few words today. Lillie Mae Liles. Come on up."

Heads turn, and I feel like I have a thousand pairs of eyes boring holes into the back of my head. Wyatt's eyes go wide. When I reach the stage, Scully gives me a strange look. I keep my head down and approach the podium.

I clear my throat. "Um, I asked to speak today because I am also responsible for what happened to Casey Culver." The room buzzes with noise, and groups of kids lean over and whisper to each other.

"When Casey first moved here, she became instant friends with my best friend, and I was jealous. I went to Violet with a plan to make Casey wanna move back to Atlanta. I guess it worked because she's not at school today."

Mary Olivia sits with both hands covering her mouth, her eyes as big as the tires on our tractor.

"But something happened. Me and Casey became friends, and she's one of the kindest people I've ever known. She would never do anything to hurt anyone else." Tears fill my eyes, and I choke back sobs.

"Casey has a disease called leukemia which isn't contagious at all. What she needs is our help, our support, and our friendship. I wish I would've done that first. I'm here today to tell everyone I'm sorry for what I did to a friend. I wish Casey was here today so I could tell her in person."

As I step away from the podium, the silence in the gym is deafening.

Chapter 24 The Winner Is...

I don't see Mary Olivia the rest of the day. She may have gone home after my confession speech. Not that I blame her. I wish I could go home too.

I sink in my seat and put my head down on the desk as Coach Joe rattles on about eating healthy foods for vitamins and nutrition. Considering I ruined my friend's life, what I eat and don't eat doesn't matter right now. When the loudspeaker blares, I jump in my seat. The jitters are getting to me.

"Hello, students of Peachtree Junior High." Mrs. Davenport's chirpy voice sounds like the robin that wakes me up each morning. "The results of your votes are in. Thank you all for voting. This year's class president winner is...Violet Holt. Congratulations Violet."

Two girls in the back of the classroom squeal with delight. The football player up front gives a thumbs up. No one else seems to care. I moan and put my head back down on my desk. Poor Scully. I feel bad for him. Then again, I don't think he ever had a chance.

Violet Holt really does rule the school.

It doesn't even matter anymore that Violet won. What matters is making things right with Casey. When the dismissal bells rings, I shoot out of my seat like a bat out of a cave. Standing at my locker, I wait for Scully, fully expecting that smile of his to be erased from his face. Instead, a group of gagging girls follows him like sheep to a shepherd.

He tells jokes like it's the best day of his life while I'm sulking in my sorrow. He winks at the girls.

"See y'all later," he waves.

His accent hasn't improved one bit, and the girls giggle. I shake my head in wonder.

"Hey there, Lillie Mae."

His Southern accent is like fingernails scraping against chicken wire. I can't help but laugh. "Looks like you have quite a following."

A smile fills his face. "Must be the accent."

"No. It's definitely not the accent," I reply, shaking my head back and forth. I stare down at my feet, unable to look him in the eye. "Sorry about the election. I should've told you about Violet."

He shrugs. "That's okay. I still had fun. I never really cared whether I won. I wanted to get to know the kids in school. And it worked, thanks to you."

"I don't think I helped. Working with me made it worse for you."

"That's not true, Lillie."

"Yes it is." My voice quivers, and I wonder how he can still be nice when I cost him the election.

"It's not your fault I lost the election," he offers, as if reading my thoughts. "Everyone knew Violet would win no matter who ran against her."

I furrow my brows together. "It's not right."

Scully shrugs his shoulders. "Sometimes that's just the way it is. I'm not upset, so you shouldn't be either." He steps closer. "Lillie. You need to tell Casey the truth."

"I tried so many times, but I can't get the words out," I say.

"She needs to hear it from you."

"I know." My whole body shakes with fright. "What if she doesn't wanna talk to me?"

"I'm sure she's upset, but telling the truth is always the right thing to do."

I offer him a slight smile. "You sound like Jesse."

Scully gives me his award-winning grin. "Yeah. He's rubbed off on me."

In that moment, I knew what I had to do.

Chapter 25 When Sorry Isn't Enough

I tiptoe to the kitchen where Mama cooks fried chicken on the stove. The smell of sweet cornbread in the oven makes my mouth salivate. When Meemaw spots me, she grins ear to ear and winks at me. I guess that's how it is with grandmothers. Meemaw loves me no matter what I do wrong.

"Lillie Mae. Grab me the salt, will ya?" Meemaw barks.

Mama's head peers over her shoulder. The pan of hot grease on the stove heats the room, and the smell makes my hunger swell even more.

"What do you need, Lillie?" Mama asks.

"I need to talk to Casey. Will you drive me over there? Please?" I beg.

Mama turns back to the stove. "You can ride Billy's bike."

The shock of her answer feels like needles pricking my nerves. Billy's old rickety bike has a rusty chain from being left outside too long, and the pedals get stuck if you go too fast. One of these days, the chain will break, the brakes will fail, or a tire will come flying off. There's nothing worse, but it sounds like I don't have a choice.

When I stay quiet, Mama turns around. "Did you hear me, Lillie Mae?"

"Yes, ma'am." I shuffle out of the kitchen feeling sorry for myself. This has been the worst day of my life.

Trampling up the hill, I sneak a peek at the kittens inside the barn. They've grown so much, and I long to hold them again. Billy's blue bike leans against the side of our red wooden barn. I check the tires for air, then throw my leg over the seat and start to pedal. I pass my baseball field where my brothers practice pitching. Billy calls out to me, but I ignore him and keep pedaling.

I ride on Highway Nine, gazing at the pine trees laying in the red clay, their timber being sold to paper factories. I stare at what was once Short Stop's home, now leveled for a shopping mall, and wonder if evicting Short Stop's family from their farm is one of the things Duke meant when he said he had regrets.

Two eighteen-wheeler trucks filled with chicken cages pass me. The smell hits my nostrils, and I gag. My bike shakes and I weave into the lane as a Ford truck lays on his horn.

"Watch where you're going," the driver shouts out the window.

The blare of his horn scares me so bad, I jerk the tires and land on my side in a ditch with my bike on top of me. Stunned, I push the bike off and stand up. I brush dirt off my pants and get back on the bike.

When I see Major's Drugstore, I'm relieved to have made it to the square alive. I hop onto the sidewalk, and pedal as fast as I can. Passing Mary Olivia's farm, a sense of dread washes over me, and I wonder if I've lost my best friend for good this time.

When I reach Casey's house, I step off my bike and open the gate that leads to her front door. I rehearse for the hundredth time what I want to say, silently praying the words will come out. I fiddle with the rusty kickstand, then give up when it won't move, and opt for setting the bike against the brick wall. I walk up the three steps, feeling like I'm carrying a heavy load of chicken feed, knock on the door, and hold my breath.

Mrs. Culver opens the door dressed in a black dress with black high-heeled pumps. I wonder if she's in mourning for Casey. Fully expecting her to shake her finger in my face and shout at me, I cower. Instead, her soft, gentle tone surprises me.

"Hello."

I look up. Her eyes are kind, giving me the courage I need to go forward. "Is Casey home? I'd really like to talk to her."

Mrs. Culver opens the door wider and steps to the side. "Come in, Lillie Mae." I step into the family room. Once bursting with laughter, it's now silent and cold. "Have a seat. I'll go get her."

Mrs. Culver points to the striped couch on the other side of the room, but I can't make my feet move. My heart pounds, and my head aches. When Casey steps into the room, I take a deep breath. Her hair is pulled back into a messy bun, and she wears pink pajamas. She doesn't smile, and neither do I. We both stand there, waiting for the other one to speak first.

"Hey," I manage to squeak out.

"Hi." Casey sits on the couch and lets out a loud sigh like she'd been holding her breath for a while. "I heard about your speech."

"You did?" I lift my eyebrows, feeling hopeful for the first time in days.

"Mary Olivia told me what you said."

Tears fill my eyes. "I'm so sorry, Casey. I didn't mean for any of this to happen. It was a horrible thing to do."

Casey puts her head in her hands and sobs. "I thought I got away from all this when I moved here."

I inch in closer. "I was so jealous of you because Mary Olivia was *my* best friend before you came to town. Then, I got to know you and realized you are fun and nice. You became my other best friend."

Casey looks up, tears streaming down her cheeks. "*This* is how you treat your best friends?"

"No! I mean, when I came up with the stupid idea that I wanted you to move back to Atlanta, I hardly knew you. Once we became friends, I refused to go along with Violet's plan, but she wouldn't listen." I grunt, feeling frustrated. "Oh, this is not what I wanted to say."

"Well, what did you come to say?" Casey's tone is tense.

"That I'm sorry for everything I said about you. I'm sorry I thought bad things about you. And mostly, I'm sorry I hurt you. I don't want you to move, and I wanna make things right. I hope one day, you'll forgive me and we can be friends again."

I hang my head and shuffle my feet on the ground, unsure what to do next. When I look up, Casey flees the room without a word. Sensing that's my cue to leave, I walk to the front door when Mrs. Culver stops me.

"Lillie Mae, wait." Slowly, I turn around to face her, wondering what she will say. "Thank you for coming and for apologizing. That took a lot of courage."

My voice catches in my throat. "I wish sayin' I'm sorry was enough."

"Lillie," Mrs. Culver pauses. "There's something you should know. A few days before all this happened with Violet, and well, with you, Casey found out her leukemia had returned. She was going to tell you that day."

The air goes out of my lungs, and I feel dizzy as the room spins. I lose my balance and Mrs. Culver places her hand below my elbow to steady me. "No!"

She leads me to the kitchen and helps me into a chair where I collapse, my head falling into my hands. "Can she come back to school?" I whisper, glancing up at her.

Mrs. Culver's expression is sad. "Not this week. We'll be at the cancer center in Atlanta for a few days. I hope she can return next week."

I look up at her, my eyes watery. "My youngest sister, Grace, has been sick since she was born. She almost died last summer."

"I'm sorry to hear that."

"She has asthma, which is usually okay, but sometimes it gets really bad, and we have to take her to the hospital."

"It's hard watching someone you love suffer, isn't it?" Mrs. Culver whispers.

I nod. "Yes, ma'am. That's why I'm tellin' you this." My eyes fill with tears as I stand to face her. "What can I do?"

Mrs. Culver puts her hands on my shoulders and looks me straight in the eye. "She needs her friends to help her through this, Lillie Mae. I know, when the time is right, you'll be there for her."

Chapter 26 🍊 Making Things Right

As I climb back onto the bike for the long journey home, I can't help pondering what I would do if I found out I had leukemia. I've never known anyone who had cancer before, so I don't know how to help Casey. But I promised her I would make things right, and that's what I intend to do.

After pedaling for what feels like hours, I reach my driveway. I stop at Meemaw and Pappy's, hoping they can help me. Laying the bike in the grass, I climb the stairs and knock on the front door.

When Pappy answers, he raises his eyebrows in surprise. "Lillie Mae? Ya all right?"

"Yes, sir. May I come in?"

"Of course." He steps aside. "Edith? Lillie Mae's here."

I walk into the familiar family room. Its warmth lifts my spirits. Their blue flowered couch, the picture of Mama and Daddy in a frame, and the smell of meatloaf cooking give me a sense of comfort. I wrap my arms around my waist, hugging my body to keep it from coming apart.

Meemaw comes around the corner with a lacy yellow apron tied around her waist. When she sees me, she darts toward me and pulls me into a bear hug. "What is it, child? What's wrong?"

I've never figured out how Meemaw and Pappy both know the instant something is wrong. "I just came from Casey's house," I say, dropping my head.

Meemaw motions toward the blue couch. "Sit down and tell us what happened." Meemaw sits next to me, and Pappy stands across the room.

"It's worse than I thought. Casey's cancer has come back." Tears fall down my cheeks. "The problem is, I did a horrible thing, Meemaw. I don't think Casey will ever forgive me."

I fall onto Meemaw's lap, and she strokes my head. "We all do bad things sometimes. Ya know, Lillie Mae, most folks would never do what you did—admit the truth and say you're sorry. You're more grown than most adults."

I don't know about that. I don't feel grownup right now.

Pappy smiles. "Meemaw and I are proud of ya, Lillie. Ain't we, Edith?"

"Sure are." Meemaw squeezes my shoulder.

"Y'all will be friends again. You'll see." Pappy smiles.

"I don't know, Pappy. She's really upset with me."

Pappy crosses the room and sits on the other side of me. "She'll be all right, Lillie Mae. You did the right thing."

I place the back of my head against the soft fabric of the couch. "I promised I'd make it right, but I don't know how."

"Be a good friend, like I know ya can," Meemaw says, rubbing her fingers through my hair. "Show her what a good friend is like. She'll come around." Meemaw squeezes me so tight, I feel the blood draining out of me.

Then it hits me like a lightning bolt. "I got it."

"Got what?" Pappy hollers.

"I know what I gotta do." Hugging Meemaw and Pappy, I leap out of my seat and bolt for the back door, shouting over my shoulder. "Thank you. Love you."

I'm out the door in a flash. Leaving the bike behind, I run across the baseball field and fly inside my house as Mama sets mashed potatoes on the table. Once everyone sits down to supper, Daddy says the blessing. He thanks God for our many blessings and for the health of our family. When he's done, my brothers chatter about baseball, football, and who knows what else. I stay silent, barely touching my food.

"How did it go at Casey's?" Ellie whispers.

I drop my fork, making a loud clanging noise, and announce, "I wanna have a family meeting."

In my household, family meetings are a regular part of our lives. There's so many of us that sometimes it takes a meeting to get everyone on the same page. Mama and Daddy are in charge of family meetings, so seeing the shock on my sibling's faces would be downright hilarious under other circumstances.

Daddy furrows his eyebrows, forming a crease in the middle of his forehead. "Lillie Mae. What's this about?"

"It's a matter of life and death. Casey needs our help."

Chapter 27 A Good Friend

After supper, I call Meemaw and Pappy on the phone and beg them to come over, not giving them much explanation. When they arrive, Ellie and I squish together in a yellow chair in our family room, and Grace sits cross-legged on the floor at Ellie's feet. Mama and Daddy take a seat side-by-side on the yellow and blue flowered couch. My brothers scatter all around the room.

"Do we have to do this now?" Billy whines. "I wanna play baseball. Jimmy said I could be the pitcher."

"Hush, Billy," Meemaw warns. "This is important to your sister."

"So. It's not important to me," Billy complains.

"Enough, Billy," Daddy barks. "Let Lillie Mae talk. What's on your mind, Lillie?"

Since everyone knows all the things I've done wrong, I don't start from the beginning. I begin with what I've just learned. "Casey's cancer has come back."

"What?" Ellie's face registers utter shock.

Mama's jaw drops, and Jimmy's lip quivers. He looks away, but not before I see him wipe his eyes.

"Is she gonna die?" Grace's voice shakes.

"No, Grace." I pat her on the shoulder.

Ellie's eyes fill with tears. "Grace and I read *Little Women* last night. Now I know why Casey was so upset when we were talking about the book."

Grace chokes back the tears. "Lillie. In the book...Beth dies."

I reach down and squeeze Grace's shoulders and smile. "That's not gonna happen to Casey because we're gonna help."

Billy stares at me like I'm crazy. "Why are *we* gonna help?"

Jimmy flicks Billy in the head. "Because she's sick. Duh."

Billy throws his hand to his head. "Ouch."

"Boys. That's enough," Mama scolds.

Ignoring Billy, I continue. "I learned somethin' today." I glance at Jesse sitting on the floor near Pappy. "I think I'm supposed to learn how to be a good friend."

Jesse grins ear to ear. "That's good, Lil. That's real good."

George slumps on the floor next to Grace, and he throws his head back against my legs. "Did Casey ask for help?"

"No." I ruffle George's hair. "But that's what a good friend does. Helps even when the person doesn't ask for it."

Mama smiles. "I'm proud of you, Lillie."

I puff up. "I wanna raise money to help pay for her treatments."

Mama crosses one arm over her waist and places the other on her chin. "Um, Lillie. That is really kind, but I don't think the Culver's need money. They're um..." She pauses, trying to gather her words. "They're quite well-off financially."

I stare at her. "You told me to make things right, Mama, and that's what I'm gonna do. They may not *need* the money, but I can't think of a nicer way to show how much we care."

Daddy smiles. "She has a point, Ruth. We tell the kids all the time to be kind and givin'. The town showed support for us when we needed it the most. This can be our way of givin' back."

"You're right, Tommy Ray." Mama plants a kiss on Daddy's cheek.

"Ew, gross." George buries his head in his hands.

Daddy chuckles. "Besides, looks can be deceiving."

Mama tilts her head to the side. "What do you mean?"

"Everyone figured they are well-off on account of how they dress," Daddy answers. "Turns out, Casey's illness has left them in tremendous debt. They don't want anyone knowin', since they lived in the rich part of Atlanta."

"Well, all be..." Meemaw shakes her head. "All the more reason we need to help."

"Whacha got in mind, Lil?" Jesse asks.

Clearing my throat, I sit up nice and tall in the chair. "I was thinking we could do a bake sale. I can ask Uncle Chicken if we can have it at The Mill."

"Good idea," Ellie chimes in. "Our friends can help us make things to sell."

Jimmy turns to Daddy. "How much money do you think they could raise?"

Daddy twists his jaw. "Probably not much. Depends how many folks show up. You'll need to get the word out quickly."

I leap off the chair, knocking George over sideways. "We don't have much time. Saturday is only four days away."

"Ya wanna do this on Saturday?" Pappy tilts his head to the side. "I don't suppose that's enough time to pull this off."

Meemaw elbows him. "Of course it is, William. If Lillie Mae wants to do this by Saturday, then I gotta get bakin'." She stands up and straightens her skirt. "William, go get me some flour from Sawyer's. I've got peach pies to make."

Pappy chuckles. "Lillie Mae. I reckon your personality came straight from your Meemaw."

Daddy laughs out loud. "You got that right."

Chapter 28 ● The Old Twin

Pappy and I hop into his Ford truck and head to The Mill to see Uncle Chicken. It's almost dark by the time we arrive, and most of the workers have left. I jump out of the cab and dash inside, hoping Uncle Chicken hasn't left yet.

"Uncle Chicken?" I shout.

"Back here," he hollers.

I run to his office in the back of the building and find him bent over a black metal file cabinet. "Well, if it ain't the old twin," he says, without looking. He chuckles as he turns around.

My eyes go wide. "How did you know it was me?"

"Same way I know the answers to the math problems ya give me. Ya haven't stumped me yet, now have ya?"

I laugh. "No, sir. But I'm gonna keep tryin'."

"Atta girl. Whatcha doin' here?"

"I need to ask you an important question. Can me and my friends have a bake sale here this Saturday?"

He drops his keys on the metal cabinet, the clanging noise echoing throughout the warehouse. "Whatcha wanna do that for?"

"It's a long story." I let out a loud puff.

"Ya got yourself into some sort of trouble again?"

Feeling defeated, my shoulders slump. "Yes, sir. But I'm tryin' to make things right. I hurt my friend, and now all I want is for her to see what a true friend can be."

Uncle Chicken scrunches up his nose. "What's that gotta do with a bake sale?"

"I wanna raise money to help Casey fight her leukemia. I figure if she sees how much people care about her, she won't move back to Atlanta."

Uncle Chicken scratches his head with one hand. "Why would she move back to Atlanta?"

My head hangs low. "Because everyone at school thinks she's contagious." I lift my head and look him straight in the eye. "But she's not—contagious, I mean. She good and kind and nice and, well, I wanna help."

Uncle Chicken rubs his gums together and leans against his desk. "I see." He doesn't say anything else for several seconds, and for once, I keep my mouth shut. "Is yur Meemaw gonna bake her famous peach pie?"

My eyes light up. "Yes, sir. Pappy and me are on the way to Sawyer's right now to buy flour."

"Um, um. Well, in that case. Ya can have it here."

I throw my arms around his waist. "Thank you, Uncle Chicken."

He chuckles his silent laugh. "Now get goin'. I gotta lock up."

"Yes, sir." I twist on my heels and call over my shoulder, "See you Saturday."

When Pappy and I pull up to Sawyer's, the lights go out.

"Oh no. We're too late," I cry, disappointed.

Pappy opens his door and saunters toward the building. "Nah. Rumsfeld knows we're comin'."

"He does?" I step out of the Ford and slam the old rickety door.

"Yep. Telephoned him before we left. Gotta make Meemaw proud of me somehow." Pappy winks at me.

"Oh, Pappy." I giggle.

"Come on. We gotta hurry."

I follow him inside where Mr. Rumsfeld greets us at the door. "Hey there, young lady." He sticks his hand out and shakes hands with Pappy.

"I'm Lillie Mae, in case you weren't sure," I offer. Most folks can't tell Ellie and me apart any more than two white ducks in a row.

"Good to see you, Lillie Mae. Let me get that flour for you, William."

Once we pay Mr. Rumsfeld for the flour, Pappy and I hop back in his truck and head home. My plan is coming together. "Thanks for helpin' me, Pappy."

He grins. "You're a good friend, Lillie Mae."

Chapter 29 Sour Lemon and Sweet Tea

Mama allows Ellie and me to stay up late making flyers for the bake sale. We use sheets of white lined paper and write all the information in block letters, including the time and place. Grace colors each paper with her crayons, doing her best to stay inside the lines.

When Jesse offers to help, I waste no time having him make large signs announcing the event. Pappy promised he'd post them all over Triple Gap and in the next town over.

Jimmy, Billy, and George aren't around, but I don't mind. I know they care in their own way—especially Jimmy. I could tell it upset him. It must be hard to hear the girl you're crushing on is sick.

Grace lies on her stomach with her feet in the air, coloring every paper Ellie and I throw her way. Mama pokes her head around the wall from the kitchen. "Girls, it's getting late. You can finish up tomorrow. Grace, go brush your teeth. It's way past your bedtime."

"Aw, Mama," Grace whines. "I wanna stay up."

"There will be plenty of work you can do tomorrow."

Grace kicks her heels together in the air and drops her pink crayon. Ellie tickles Grace under the arms, making her giggle and dart out of the room.

I snicker. "That's one way to get her up."

Ellie yawns. "I can't keep my eyes open."

Her yawn is contagious. "Me either." I stack the flyers together and count. "Twenty-five. Well, it's a start. We can pass these out at school, then make more tomorrow night."

"Let's get Sarah and Mary Olivia to help us," Ellie suggests.

I stand up and walk toward our room. "Mary Olivia doesn't want to be friends with me anymore. She hates me."

"She doesn't hate you. She's upset."

Changing into my pajamas, I stroll to the bathroom to brush my teeth. "I would hate me too if I were her."

"She doesn't *hate* you," Ellie stresses, squeezing toothpaste onto her toothbrush. "You and Mary Olivia have been friends since third grade. She knows what you're like."

With my toothbrush still stuffed in my mouth, I spit toothpaste into the sink. "What's that supposed to mean?"

Ellie shrugs. "You're a Sour Lemon. Always have been. You get yourself tangled up more than an insect in a spider web, but you always come around." Unsure what to say, I rinse my toothbrush. "I should read you something from *Little Women*."

"That old book, again?" I groan.

"You mean that classic," Ellie corrects.

I roll my eyes and dry my face with the towel. Ellie and I say goodnight to Mama and Daddy before heading to our room. Ellie grabs the classic off the dresser as I lie down on her bed. She thumbs through the pages looking for the story and babbles on about Mrs. Marsh and the four sisters.

"Jo asked her mother to tell a story with a moral to it. Here it is. In chapter four." Ellie turns the page and reads quietly so she won't wake up Grace.

"*Once upon a time, there were four girls, who had enough to eat and drink and wear, a good many comforts and pleasures, kind friends and parents, who love them dearly, and yet were not contented.*"

I furrow my eyebrows together. "What's that got to do with me?"

"Shh," Ellie says. "Let me finish." She moves her finger along the words on the page, finds her place, and reads.

"*The girls were anxious to be good, and made many excellent resolutions; but they did not keep them very well, and were constantly saying, 'If we only had this,' or 'If we could only do that,' quite forgetting how much they already had, and how many pleasant things they actually could do. So they asked an old woman what spell they could use to make them happy, and she said, 'When you feel discontented, think over your blessings and be grateful.'*"

Ellie looks up from the book and sighs. "Sometimes you can't see what's right in front of you."

"What's that supposed to mean?" I ask, unsure whether I should be insulted.

Ellie shuts the book and hops off the bed. She sets it on the dresser, then plops down next to me. "It means you had a good friend and the opportunity to make a new friend, but you let your jealousy get the best of you. Not everything's gonna go your way every time. Be thankful for what you have, instead of worrying about what you don't have."

Ellie's right and I hug her, smudging leftover toothpaste onto her white nightgown. I brush it off with my hand.

"I'm still tryin' to be Sweet Tea like you."

Ellie giggles quietly. "I know. And you will be—one day." She yawns. "When lemons come your way, you eventually make lemonade. Maybe you should try that first next time."

Smiling, I climb the ladder to my bunk bed, exhausted. Before collapsing on the pillow, I lean my head over the side. "Thanks for helping me today."

Ellie yawns again. "That's what twins are for."

Even though I'm more tired than a hound dog after a coon hunt, I can't sleep. There are so many things on my mind. I sit up in bed and say a silent prayer.

"Dear God. I'm sorry about being such a bad friend to Casey. Help me be thankful for what I have and stop messing things up. Please help Casey and Mary Olivia forgive me. And please let this bake sale work so Casey can get better."

Chapter 30   Besties

The next morning, I dread running into Mary Olivia at school. Rather than chance bumping into her, I make a beeline for my locker. Scully shuffles toward me, surrounded by a group of eighth-grade girls.

"Yes, yes, girls. I promise I'll *try* to get better food in the cafeteria. I'll work my magic." He winks at each of them as echoes of "ah's" fill the air. The fluttering of eyelashes is enough to make me head for the hen houses.

When he reaches my locker, he pushes the girls aside. "Hey, y'all. It's my best friend, Lillie Mae." He smiles big and proud.

The girls mutter to themselves, and I'm embarrassed. "Hey, Scully," I whisper, keeping my head down.

"Ya need to turn that frown upside down," he screeches in his horrid Southern accent. One girl giggles at his joke, and I can't help myself. I laugh with her. Scully has a way of making me feel better without even trying.

"You're crazy, Scully Scrub," I say, shaking my head.

He drops the Southern accent. "Maybe I am, but at least you're smiling."

I hand him a flyer. Before his flock of geese flies away, I hand them flyers too and explain my plan.

Scully lifts his eyebrows, making his forehead wrinkle, and reads aloud. "A bake sale raising money for Casey Culver will take place at The Mill Saturday October twentieth. We will present Casey with her gift Saturday night." He looks up at me. "You did all this in one day?"

"Yep. That's what friends are for."

"Wow, Lillie Mae. Count me in to help. And Wyatt too. What can we do?"

"Can you help Jesse make more signs?" I ask.

"Sure. I'll go find Wyatt." He takes two steps before turning back around. "That's really nice, what you're doing for Casey."

My face curves into a slight smile. "Thanks, but I should've tried being nice first."

I slam my locker and spin on my heels. Mary Olivia stands in front of me, her expression hard to read. She holds out a flyer, and for a second, I think she's going to shove it in my face.

Mary Olivia looks down at her feet, then glances up at me with tear-filled eyes. "I've been so mad at you, Lillie Mae. Then you got up on stage and told the whole school the truth." She pauses. "You're brave and strong. Stronger than I'll ever be."

I move my head back and forth. "That's not true. I'm not brave at all." I work up the courage to look her in the eye. "You're a better friend."

She shakes her head, and her hair sticks to her pink lip-gloss. "That's not true, either. If I had been a good friend to you, none of this would have happened."

"What do you mean? I made this mess."

"Yeah, but it's my fault too. I was so excited when Casey wanted to be friends with me." She glances away. "You know—the country girl from the farm—that I made you feel like you weren't special. But you are. Special, I mean."

Mary Olivia pulls me into a hug, and my body goes limp. I can't believe she can forgive me after what I've done. I guess God was listening after all. Slowly, my arms reach around her, and we stand like that for what feels like hours.

"Are y'all gonna hug all day?" Wyatt stands with his arms crossed as Mary Olivia and I separate.

Embarrassed by my tears, I look away. "Hey, Wyatt."

"You crying again, Lillie Mae?" he asks.

"No," I lie.

"Good. 'Cause from what I hear, we got a bake sale to plan."

Mary Olivia grins and tilts her head sideways. "Wyatt, did you know I make the best chocolate chip cookies this side of the Mississippi?"

"Nope," Wyatt answers.

"It's true," I say, sniffling. "She really does. You better come to the bake sale with your wallet full."

Wyatt smiles, and I smile back. His sandy blond hair falls in his face, making his brown eyes sparkle. We stand there grinning at each other as time stands still.

"Okay, you lovebirds," Mary Olivia barks, interrupting the best moment of my life. "Enough of that googly eye stuff. Let's go to class." Mary Olivia throws her arm over my shoulder.

Looks like I got my best friend back.

Chapter 31 Asking for Help

Mary Olivia and Sarah come over after school to help me plan the bake sale. Ellie gets white-lined paper, and the four of us write all the information folks need to provide baked goods. Once we've colored another fifty flyers, my fingers curve into fists and won't straighten.

Pappy drives us to the square to hand out flyers. Mary Olivia and Sarah skirt off to Major's Drugs, so I head to the bank. Not wanting to face Mr. Holt alone, I drag Ellie with me.

The bell jingles when Ellie opens the door, and the lady behind the check counter smiles. "Good afternoon, girls." Her head swishes side to side as she processes Ellie and me. "Twins?"

No. We just look exactly the same.

Thank goodness Ellie speaks up first. "Yes, ma'am. We'd like to leave a few flyers here for your customers if we may." Ellie steps to the counter and hands the lady a paper.

She looks it up and down and smiles. "Sure. Why don't you place them over there, next to the deposit slips?" She points to a long table in the center of the room.

I muster some courage and take a deep breath. "Is Mr. Holt here?"

"Yes, he's in his office. Would you like me to get him for you?"

"Yes, please." I shuffle my feet on the carpet and wrap my arms around my waist.

The lady goes to the back and comes back in an instant. "He'll be right out."

A few seconds later, a booming voice behind me resonates. "Lillie Mae?"

Whipping my entire body around, I look up at Duke Holt. "Hey, Mr. Holt. Can me and Ellie talk with you for a minute?"

"Sure. Follow me."

He leads us to his office and gestures to the enormous brown chairs. He leaves the door open, and walks around his gigantic wooden desk and sits down. Ellie and I lower ourselves into the leather chairs. Feeling small, I sit forward in my seat.

"What can I do for you?" His deep blue eyes are intimidating.

"I did what you said, Mr. Holt. I took responsibility for my mistake."

"Yes, I know," he says. "I heard your speech."

"Yeah, but not just that. I went to Casey and apologized. Now, I'm trying to help her."

Ellie hands him a flyer. "We're tryin' to raise money to help Casey with her cancer treatments, and we were wonderin' if you can help?" Her voice is as sweet as honey.

Mr. Holt falls back in his chair, swivels to the right, and scratches his chin. He reads the flyer before handing it back to Ellie. "Not sure I'm too good at baking." His face curves into a slight smile, and his eyes sparkle.

Ellie grins. "Oh, well, it's not baked items we need. We want to let folks know about the bake sale, and we were hopin' you could help."

"I could do that."

I wait for him to say something else, only he doesn't. Stuttering, I manage to get a few words out. "O-o-okay. Thank you. Can you please let your customers know to come to The Mill on Saturday?"

He nods. "I'll do that."

Ellie clears her throat. "Well, thank you for your time and for helpin' us, Mr. Holt."

I flee the room and whisper to Ellie as we walk to the door, "Did we make a mistake askin' him for help?"

"I'm not sure," she says, her voice shaky.

Chapter 32   Sweet Treats

When Friday rolls around, it's time to finish baking for tomorrow's sale. I hop off the bus and run to Meemaw's house to check on her pies. Pappy waits for me on the porch, like he does most days.

He hollers as I approach. "Y'all have a good day at school?"

"Yes, sir," Jesse announces.

"We learned a lot," Jimmy bellows before Pappy can ask.

Pappy laughs so hard, he grabs his belly. "Well, I'll be. It's about time."

I leap up the steps, two-by-two. "Jimmy got ya, didn't he Pappy?" I crash into him, my braids hitting his shaking belly.

"Sure did." He chuckles.

I muster the most serious face I can, and lower my voice to a whisper. "How are Meemaw's pies coming along? You eat them all yet?"

"No, but he tried," Meemaw barks from inside the doorway.

Pappy winks at me, and I giggle. "I came to check on your progress, Meemaw. Are you done yet?"

She ushers me through the family room and into the kitchen, leaving Pappy alone on the porch. When I round the corner, my mouth falls open. Sitting on the white Formica countertop are fifteen peach pies, all in a row.

"Meemaw!"

"I know, I know," she says. "I've outdone myself."

"You're not kidding." My mouth waters, and my stomach gurgles.

"Pappy went back to Sawyer's twice 'cause I kept on bakin'. Had to shoo him outta here more times than I can count." She shakes her head.

Throwing my arms around her waist, I hug her tight. "Thanks for helpin' me."

"Of course. It's what grandmothers do for those they love." She grins. "Your mama's been baking banana bread all day. I swear Pappy can smell it from here. I look out the window, and there he is, shufflin' over to your house, lookin' for somethin' to eat." I giggle. "You ready to start on your chocolate cupcakes?"

My tongue tingles at the thought. "Yes, ma'am. I'm gonna get Ellie, and I'll be right back."

I skip the whole way home. I can't believe how everything came together in such a short time. When I walk through my front door, the scent of fresh banana bread fills the air. My lungs expand as does my hunger. Billy and George sit at the round kitchen table with mouths full of bread. Crumbs leak from George's mouth when he tries to smile at me. Mama's loaves of banana bread fill the counter. I count eight loaves, but one has giant chucks pulled right out of the middle.

My head flips from the bread to my brothers. "Does Mama know yet?"

Billy points at George. "He started it."

"And you didn't stop him?" I scream.

He answers with a mouth full of food. "It was too late."

I grunt. "Why did you join in?"

He shrugs. "I figured we couldn't sell it. So, why not?"

"Ah," I shriek, flying out of the room.

I stomp to my bedroom and pull an old gray shirt and blue jeans out of my dresser drawer.

"Did you see Billy and George?" I ask Ellie. "They're eating one of Mama's loaves. Mama made that for Casey, not for our greedy brothers."

Ellie exhales. "Let Mama handle it. At least you're not the one in trouble this time."

I throw my arms in the air. "It's about time." I slip on my work clothes and tie my sneakers. "Come on. We've got cupcakes to make."

Ellie and I race across the baseball field and dash onto Meemaw's back porch. I don't bother knocking this time. We bound into the kitchen as Meemaw gets out flour, sugar, eggs, and vegetable oil, setting each on the countertop.

"Hey, Meemaw." Ellie says.

"Hey there, darlin'." Meemaw pulls Ellie into a hug. "Lillie Mae. Grab the cocoa powder out of the cabinet, will ya?"

"Sure." I wander to the cabinet filled with baking soda, salt, and cocoa powder. Placing all three on the counter, I shriek.

"What?" Ellie shouts.

"That," I say, pointing to the shiny, white electric mixer on the countertop. "When did you get that?"

Meemaw has had the same mixer since I was born—lime green with two silver beaters that require two hundred tons of force to squeeze into the holes. I should know since I help her make everyone's birthday cake.

Meemaw winks at me. "Pappy brought home this brand spankin' new mixer. Swore up and down it was on sale and I needed a new one to make all these pies."

Her new mixer is solid white with shiny beaters and a large glass bowl. I push the beaters in place, amazed at how easily they click into position. "I can't believe it, Meemaw."

She smiles. "Don't know what he was thinkin'. Well, we gotta get started on these cupcakes if we're gonna finish tonight."

Ellie measures the flour, baking soda, and salt while I measure the oil and sugar. When I turn the mixer on, it sends sugar crystals across the room. Ellie screams and ducks behind the table. I yank the turn handle to slow it down, only I turn it the wrong way, sending the mixer into high speed. The once cracked eggs in the bowl are now scrambled eggs across the walls.

Meemaw rushes over and cuts the switch. "Good gracious, child. What in the Sam Hill were ya thinkin'?"

I giggle. Now I know where Daddy got that expression. "Who is Sam Hill? Daddy uses that expression too."

"Never mind that. Look at the mess ya made."

A chunk of sugar-egg mixture on the cabinet above Meemaw's head falls into her gray bouffant hair. I let out a stream of giggles. Ellie cracks up, laughing even louder than me, but at least she has the decency to pull the chunk off of Meemaw's head. I'm bent over laughing with my hands on my knees.

"Clean up this mess, girls," Meemaw barks. She acts mad, but she's really not because I see the smile forming on her face as she grabs a rag from the drawer and wipes the walls. Meemaw cackles right along with her grand-chicks.

After spending the next twenty minutes cleaning the kitchen from floor to ceiling, Ellie and I begin again. This time, Meemaw turns the mixer on and off, since she won't let me touch it. Taking out the two cupcake pans, I spread shortening inside each cup, then place a small amount of flour on top. Meemaw pours in the cake batter and places the pans in a hot oven. I offer to share the leftover batter with Ellie, but she turns her nose up because she doesn't like chocolate. It's a wonder we're even twins.

I lick the bowl clean before washing it, so Ellie can start on the frosting. She pours confectioners' sugar, milk, vanilla, and shortening in the bowl. Meemaw turns the mixer on low, letting the bowl spin around in circles.

Once the two dozen cupcakes have cooled, Ellie and I spread the white frosting on each one. I dip my knife in hot water to make the frosting spread nice and smooth, then place each cupcake inside a large cardboard box that Pappy pulled out of a closet.

I sure hope folks to show up tomorrow to buy our sweet treats.

Chapter 33 🍋 Bake Sale

When my family arrives at The Mill the next morning, I'm shocked to see cars here this early. Pappy pulls up in his Ford, and he and Daddy unload three tables they borrowed from the church, and set them up in the grass. Mama and Meemaw place red and white checked tablecloths on each one.

Jimmy and Jesse help me unload Meemaw's pies and my cupcakes. Ellie arranges them on the tables as I direct folks to the bake sale. Before long, we have three tables full of fudge, cookies, pies, and cupcakes, donated from folks all across town. I thank each person as they place their donation on the table. The town came together for Casey, and I can't wait to see her face when we surprise her.

When I spot Mary Olivia, I run to greet her. Her arms are full of homemade chocolate chip cookies, and my mouth waters.

"I want to eat them all now," I say.

"Better not. I'm selling them for twenty-five cents each." She laughs and places them on the table next to my cupcakes.

Our first customer of the day is Uncle Chicken. He waves. "Hey there, old twin."

"I'm not old yet, Uncle Chicken." I laugh. "Got a fresh pie with your name on it." I stand up, select the biggest peach pie on the table, and hand it to him.

He sniffs it. "Um, um. Yur Meemaw sure can cook. Can't wait to eat this."

I stretch out the palm of my hand toward him. "That'll be three dollars, please."

Uncle Chicken chuckles. "Ya don't miss a beat, do ya?"

I shake my head. "No, sir. Gotta raise a lot of money today."

He fumbles through his pockets and pulls out a money-clip. He slips a five-dollar bill off the top and hands it to me. "Keep the change."

My eyes go wide, and I run around the table and throw my arms around his waist. "Thank you, Uncle Chicken."

"Well, my goodness. No need to fuss." Uncle Chicken pats me on the back.

Ellie grins ear to ear as I hand her a crisp five-dollar bill. "Thanks, Uncle Chicken."

Dropping my arms, I run back to my place behind the table as he saunters back to The Mill. As folks arrive, Grace directs them from the parking lot down the hill to Ellie and me. Ellie takes the money, and I hand each person their sweet treat and a flyer.

"Don't forget about tonight. Come if you can," I repeat to everyone who walks by.

When all of my cupcakes sell, I puff up like a peacock. Mary Olivia spends her time getting folks to buy her cookies. Meemaw's pies are almost gone when Doctor Hardy bounds down the hill chatting with Mama. Doctor Hardy used to come to our house when The Twins, George and Grace, were born. He's been taking care of Grace ever since. She adores him and drags him down the hill to buy our sweet treats.

"Doctor Hardy wants one of Meemaw's pies." Grace smiles.

He chuckles. "*Famous* peach pie from what I hear."

"Looks like you're just in time," Ellie replies. "You got the last one."

"Well. They must be good. I'll take it."

"Three-dollars, please." I stick out my hand.

Doctor Hardy hands me a twenty-dollar bill, and I pass it to Ellie. When Ellie reaches into the jar to count out his change, he stops her. "I don't need change. That'll be my donation."

My jaw drops. "Wow. Thank you, sir."

Mama furrows her eyebrows. "Are you sure? That's a lot of money."

"I'm sure, Ruth." He turns from Mama to Ellie and me. "I hope it can help that sweet girl."

Ellie tilts her head to the side. "You know Casey?"

"Yes, from working up at the hospital." Doctor Hardy scratches his chin. "Awful her cancer came back."

I clear my throat. "Um, Doctor Hardy. How much does it cost to cure leukemia?"

"Well, there really isn't a cure yet."

I tilt my head, giving him a sideways glance. "Why not?"

"Scientists haven't been able to find one," he replies.

It makes me sad to think about Casey not having a cure. "Well, how much does it cost to get better?"

He shrugs his shoulders. "Depends. Most folks have insurance to help with the cost, but it can cost thousands of dollars. Especially for the Culvers, since they're still paying for Casey's first treatment." He looks down at his feet, shuffling them in the dirt. "Sure is a shame."

Ellie pats the money jar. "Good thing we have a lot of money for her."

Doctor Hardy grins. "It's real nice what you girls are doing for your friend."

I hand him a flyer. "Come tonight if you can, okay?"

He glances down at the paper. "I'd like that very much."

Mama smiles. "Thank you again for coming. It was mighty kind of you."

"Yeah, thanks again for your donation," Ellie adds.

When Doctor Hardy strolls back to his car, I glance at Mama. "I know what I'm going to do when I grow up."

Mama raises her eyebrows. "Really? What?"

"I'm going to cure leukemia."

Chapter 34 Counting Change

When we arrive home, Ellie and I race to the kitchen and spill the money jar onto the round table. The coins make a loud clanging noise against the wood. I separate the bills from the coins, and push a pile toward Grace.

"Here. You count the coins," I tell her.

She beams. "Okay. How much is this one?" She points to the dime.

Before I can answer, George flies into the room and lifts a five-dollar bill off the table.

"Stop it, George," I shriek. "Mama. George is taking our money."

Mama appears in the doorway, tugging George back into the kitchen. "Put it back."

"Aw," he whines, slamming the money down next to Ellie.

"Go on, now. Leave the girls be." Mama shoos him out of the room.

"We must have a thousand dollars in here." I keep counting the bills, and the numbers get higher and higher.

Ellie giggles. "It's so exciting."

Grace separates the quarters, dimes, nickels, and pennies into piles. Before anyone catches him, George sneaks back into the kitchen and snatches a quarter from Grace's pile.

"George Liles," she shouts. "You get back here this instant."

I burst out laughing. "You sound like Mama."

"Duh." Grace rolls her eyes. "I've heard her say that to him every day of my life."

Ellie and I snicker. We're about to have a full-fledged twin giggling fit.

"Oh no you don't, girls." Grace mimics Mama's voice again. "We've got money to count."

Mama and George appear behind Grace, and Mama squeezes Grace's shoulders. "You've been listening to me, I see."

Grace giggles. "Yes, ma'am."

"George, put the quarter back on the table and apologize to your sisters."

George reaches into the front pocket of his blue jeans and slams his hand on the table. "Sorry." He scurries out of the room like a flash of light.

Mama lets out a loud sigh. "How's it going?"

"Good," Ellie smiles. "We have thousands of dollars."

Mama raises one eyebrow. "Really?"

"Oh yeah. For sure," I say, grinning ear to ear.

Mama sits down next to Grace and helps her count the coins, teaching her each amount as she goes. I write down my total, then add Ellie's and Grace's dollar amount.

"The total is...one hundred fifty-two dollars and thirty-five cents? That's it?" I drop into the chair and raise my voice. "That's not enough to cure her."

Ellie sinks into the chair next to me. "What do we do now?"

Placing my elbows on my knees, I rest my chin in my hands. "I wanted to help."

Mama sits down next to me. "Lillie Mae. The Culvers are not expecting you to pay for Casey's treatments at all, and no one expects you to cure leukemia. What you did today is the nicest thing anyone has ever done for her. Your friendship and kindness will mean more to Casey than anything."

"You think so?" I hang my head, wondering if I've done anything to help.

Mama smiles. "I know so. You have a big heart, Lillie. You took responsibility for your actions, and then you made things right. That took a lot of courage." She squeezes my shoulders. "One hundred and fifty dollars may not sound like much, but it is what's in your heart that counts."

"Yeah, Lil." I didn't see Jesse sneak into the kitchen, and his voice startles me. "You learned how to be a good friend. Now, you have to trust God to work this out. He will." Jesse smiles. "You'll see."

I frown at Jesse. "I hope you're right. I sure wish it was more."

Ellie slips her arm around my sagging shoulders. "Come on, Sour Lemon. Let's go get ready for the surprise tonight." Ellie wiggles her eyebrows up and down, making me laugh out loud.

Chapter 35 The Surprise

As I ride in the back of Daddy's truck with my brothers and sisters, the cool breeze makes my long, brown hair fly in my face. My head flips side to side at all the folks walking down Main Street toward Casey's house. I wave to Mary Olivia and Sarah walking on the sidewalk.

Wyatt and Scully cross the street behind our truck, and Wyatt waves. His hair is wet and pushed off his forehead, like he stepped out of the shower. He looks amazing.

When Daddy parks, I hop out of the bed of the truck and spot Pastor Eddie standing in Casey's front lawn with a group of folks from church. From the looks of things, half the town came to show their support.

Pastor Eddie approaches me. "There you are." He glances around. "We've been waiting for you. Ready?"

I nod my head yes, but I want to scream no. Working up the courage to ring the doorbell, I glance back at Wyatt. He smiles and nods toward the door. When I turn back around, the door pops open. Mrs. Culver stands behind her screen door, dressed in khaki bell-bottom pants and a pale yellow sweater. The jitters get the best of me, and I lose my nerve. I stand as still as a statue, speechless.

The sun peeks out from behind a white, puffy cloud, casting an orange glow on Mrs. Culver's face. She lifts her hand to shield the bright light, and her chin drops. I step backward off the porch steps, lose my balance, and fall into someone's arms. My eyes register shock as Wyatt holds me. Embarrassed, my face heats up, and I really hope those annoying red splotches don't appear on my cheeks this time.

Wyatt whispers in my ear and points to the porch where Casey stands in blue jeans and a light blue sweatshirt. Her mom and dad stand on either side of her. Wyatt gives me a slight push. "Go talk to her, Lillie."

Clearing my throat, I take two steps forward. "Hey, Casey. Um, everyone's here because we care about you."

I point to the folks behind me holding up signs for her to read. One family holds up a piece of cut cardboard with the words, "We love you Casey," painted on it. Another sign reads, "We're here for you, Casey."

Ellie stands next to me on the walkway and hands me the money jar. I take it from Ellie and hold it out toward Casey. "We had a bake sale for you today and raised over one hundred and fifty dollars. It's not enough to cover all your treatments, but we wanted to help."

Casey walks down the stairs, tears streaming down her red cheeks. Without taking the jar, she falls into me, squeezing the breath out of my lungs. "Thank you," she whispers over and over in my ear.

When she lets go, I nod toward everyone else. "I didn't do it alone. Everyone here helped. We hope you'll stay in Triple Gap. No, wait. I hope you'll stay."

Casey nods her head. "Oh, I'm definitely staying. You're the best friend a girl could ask for."

Mary Olivia, Sarah, and Ellie join our hug, and the five of us stand together until Pastor Eddie makes an announcement.

"Mr. and Mrs. Culver. Casey," he shouts above the crowd like a true preacher. "On behalf of all of those at First Baptist Triple Gap, I wanted y'all to know we will do everything we can to help you folks. The ladies of the church brought casseroles to help make this time easier for your family."

As several women step forward with meals, Mr. Culver ushers them inside the house, setting the food in the kitchen. Mrs. Culver wipes her tears, thanking each lady for coming, then walks down the stairs and pulls me into a hug.

"Lillie Mae. I knew when the time was right, you'd know what to do." Her warm eyes glow in the sunlight, filling me with happiness.

"Well, Mrs. Culver. I may make a mess of things, but God has a way of teachin' me lessons through it all." I smile, knowing Jesse will be proud of me. "Oh, I almost forgot," I shout too loud. "Jesse. Come here."

Jesse rushes to my side and hands me a Nike shoebox. It's the box from my twelfth birthday when my parents surprised me with a pair of navy blue sneakers. I place it in Casey's hands. "This is for you."

Casey's eyes widen. "Lillie. You already gave me the best gift ever."

Ellie and I giggle, and I nod toward the box. "Open it."

Casey peers into the shoebox and squeals. "Tux!"

She lifts the tiny black and white kitten out of the box, gives her a kiss, and jumps up and down. She tugs on the red-checkered bandana tied around Tux's tiny neck. She starts to say something, but I interrupt.

"We want you to have her." My family surrounds me, and I nod toward each of them. "If it's okay with your parents."

Casey runs to Mrs. Culver, her eyes pleading. "Please, Mom. Please, Daddy. Can I keep her?"

Mr. and Mrs. Culver exchange a look. After several seconds, Mrs. Culver speaks up. "Yes. You can keep her."

Casey shrieks in delight, hugging her mom and dad before rushing back to me. "Oh, Lillie, I'm so excited. Mr. and Mrs. Liles, thank you for everything."

Daddy and Mr. Culver shake hands while Mama and Mrs. Culver hug.

As Casey strokes Tux's soft fur, she turns. "By the way, why is Tux wearing a red and white checkered scarf? It's way too big for her."

My face fills with a mischievous grin. "Meemaw gave me permission to cut a piece of the tablecloth from the bake sale to make a scarf for you, in case you lose your hair and all. That way, you can still look like Daisy Duke."

Casey bursts into laughter, and Mary Olivia shouts above the crowd. "I knew it. I knew you were the *real* Daisy Duke."

"Did someone say Duke?" A loud voice booms in the evening air.

I whip my head around and come face to face with Duke Holt and Violet. Mr. Holt smiles at me.

"Lillie Mae came by my office the other day and asked if I could help. Since I'm no good at baking cookies, Violet and I hoped this would help y'all out." He motions to Violet who stretches out her hand to Casey.

"Sorry, Casey," Violet says just above a whisper. She places a piece of paper in Casey's hand. Casey's jaw drops, and she gasps for air.

Mrs. Culver looks over her shoulder and reads out loud. "One thousand dollars?" The surrounding gasps are enough to suck in all the air in Triple Gap. "Mr. Holt. I don't know what to say." Tears stream down her cheeks. "Thank you."

Mr. Holt runs his fingers through his hair. "You're welcome." He turns to face me. "This young lady has taught me a thing or two about generosity and kindness." I stare at him, unsure what to say. "Lillie Mae. Not only did you make things right with Casey, you pulled this entire town together. Again. You're quite a remarkable young lady."

Embarrassed at all the folks staring at me, I look away. "Thank you, Mr. Holt."

Daddy pats me on the head. "Our Sour Lemon is growin' up."

I place my arm around Violet's shoulders and give her a few gentle pats. "You know, Violet. You *can* be nice—when you try. Maybe you and I can be friends after all."

Violet takes my arm and throws it off of her like I've given her a disease. "Not so fast, farm girl."

Ellie and I burst out laughing. I push my shoulders up. "You can't blame a girl for tryin'."

I remember a quote from *Little Women* and clear my throat. Doing my best to recreate Jo's character, I whisper in the sweetest tone I can muster.

"*'I'll try and be what he loves to call me, 'a little woman,' and not be rough and wild...'*". I pause, forgetting the rest of the quote. "Said *Jo*."

Ellie gasps and throws her hand over her mouth. "You've been reading *Little Women*?"

"Surprised?" I ask.

Ellie's eyes widen. "Yes!"

I place both hands on my hips and grin. "I told you I was trying to be Sweet Tea."

Acknowledgements

Too many kids have been victims of bullying. Their stories inspired this book and I hope they found healing in reading Lillie's journey.

I'd like to thank my editor, Kimberly Coghlan, for the hours of hard work and the continued belief in Lillie Mae. Thank you to Sheri Williams and the TouchPoint family for the opportunity to share Lillie with the world. To my amazing launch team, I could not have done this without you. To the media specialists and teachers who made this dream become a reality. To my readers, you make me want to continue.

To my parents, Gordon and Janet, thank you for modeling faith and forgiveness. To my sisters, Kim and Tara, for believing in me. To my boys, Connor and Bryson, for sharing your mom's time and attention with those who need to hear this story. I love you both!

To my husband, Dusty, thank you for believing, encouraging, and never giving up on me. I love you with all my heart! Thank you to the Lord Jesus Christ who is the true healer of wounded hearts.

—Julane

The Sour Lemon Series
Sour Lemon and Sweet Tea, Book 1

Eleven-year-old Lillie Mae Liles plans to play baseball all summer, and why not, since she has a baseball diamond in her front yard and enough brothers and sisters to form a team. But Lillie's twin sister, bent on following the rules, thinks it is time for Lillie to grow up. As hard times hit Triple Gap, Georgia, Lillie finds herself feeding chickens that peck at her legs, growing vegetables she hates eating, and dodging insults from the richest and snobbiest girl in middle school. When Lillie spies on her parents and discovers a buried family secret, she turns her habit of spying into serious detective work. Believing that someone is trying to steal the farm, Lillie gets herself in one tangled mess after another. Can she untangle the mess she created in time to save her home? Rich in Southern humor, *Sour Lemon and Sweet Tea* is an irresistible journey of self-discovery, overcoming rejection, and the power of forgiveness.

Made in the USA
Columbia, SC
15 July 2019